THE HURRICANE KEEPER

Victoria Kimble

WALL CLOUD PRESS

For a little hurricane that blew through too quickly.

Ashlyn Grace Reid
December 3, 2015 – March 4, 2018

Chapter 1

"Hurricane Goliath shows no sign of slowing down. Since making landfall on September third, fifty years ago, the historic storm--"

"Seriously, Ashlyn? Is that what you do when you come home from school?"

I hit pause, freezing the face of the chipper meteorologist on the screen embedded in the wall of our family room. The freeze-frame had caught the poor woman with her left eye half-closed and her lips pursed like she was about to kiss the hurricane.

"It's my birthday, Trig." I stuck out my tongue at my oldest brother. "I can do whatever I want, remember? I choose the cereal, and I choose what we watch on the screen."

He flopped onto the couch. "Just three more years, Baby Sis, then you too can join America's drinking game and take a shot every time the talking heads mention September third."

I snorted. "You can't even join that game yet."

"What's five more months?"

I sat next to him and studied his face. Was he serious about becoming a regular at the bar when he turned twenty-one? I would never admit to anyone that Trig was my favorite brother. First, family is not supposed to have favorites, and second, his head would swell so big he'd never be able to fit through any doors. But when we were growing up, he never treated me like an annoying baby sister. He would let me play his VR games with him, and he was a champ at turning chores into adventures with silly songs. Him making a poor decision was my worst fear. "You're going to do shots in five months? It's so expensive. And gross. And people die from alcohol poisoning every day. Why can't you stick to the good stuff, like soda?"

Trig let out a loud laugh and grabbed my head in a headlock. "Come on, Ash. Lighten up. You don't have to worry about me."

I didn't struggle. As the youngest of four, I've learned how to navigate tricky situations. I waited until he had his fill of messing up my hair, then pinched the skin under his armpit as hard as I could. He yelped and let me go.

I smoothed my hair and settled on the couch, tucking my legs under me. "Like, when did they realize the hurricane wasn't going away?"

Trig leaned on the armrest, propping his large, smelly feet in my lap. I gagged, and his favorite status slipped a little. "I heard that back then, hurricanes blew through in a day. People had a couple of days to prepare or evacuate, but the actual hurricane only pounded them for, like, twelve hours."

I shoved his feet off my lap and resumed the video, lowering the volume and enabling the closed captions. The meteorologist had no fresh updates about the hurricane to share. Hurricane Goliath parked over Florida fifty years ago. Before Mom was born. But someday that had to change. I wanted to know the second that it did. And since living in Castle Rock, Colorado meant we were nowhere near the hurricane, I had to get my information from the peppy meteorologists on the weather app.

Three seconds later, I regretted turning down the sound. If it had been louder, I would have missed the annoying, exaggerated sigh heaved right above my head. A sigh that Trig and I heard way too often.

"Ashlyn, you are eighteen years old. How long are you going to waste money on that stupid weather app?"

I turned to Trig. "Now there's a drinking game. Do a shot every time Mella unleashes her disapproving sigh."

He stopped smiling and pushed his eyebrows together. "I thought you were worried about alcohol poisoning. If I played that game, I'd be a penniless, drunk hobo in a week."

Mella stomped over to the armchair. "Ha ha. You guys are so funny."

Trig tossed a pillow at Mella's head, which she batted away toward my face.

"You realize that if Mom canceled the app, she'd have more than enough money to buy your books for Eckman." Mella perched on the edge of the armchair rather than settling back into the cozy cushions. Every time she had something important to say, she assumed the perch-on-the-edge-of-furniture position. Which was a lot.

Trig threw another pillow. "Mel, I think you overestimate the app's price and underestimate the cost of college books."

My chest tightened as Mella and Trig squabbled about the prices of eBooks. I twisted a strand of hair around my finger and stared at the screen as the meteorologist switched radar images. Maybe I was wasting Mom's money. Maybe it was time for me to pitch in on things like this. I didn't want to delete the app, but Mella was right; Mom shouldn't have to pay for something that was so important to me. I learned long ago to stop asking why it wasn't also important to everyone else. Mr. Hart said that everyone grieves in their own way, and I shouldn't pressure anyone into participating in the things that help me cope.

I cleared my throat. "Birthday rule number eight–no fighting on my birthday. Remember?"

Mella's eyes softened. "Yeah, okay. Happy birthday."

Trig scooted over next to me, draping his huge octopus arm around my neck. "Sorry, Ash. I'll memorize all my witty retorts and recite them back to Mella later, when you're out of earshot."

I laughed, and Mella cracked a rare smile. Her grin made her face look youthful and carefree, like twenty-three-year-olds should. It wasn't easy to be the oldest in our family, and teasing her didn't help at all. Especially since, for the last five years following her high school graduation, she'd taken charge over me, Trig, and Penn so Mom could work. I didn't want to fight with her or make her sad. I glanced at the screen one more time, ready to turn it off, when something caught my eye. I tapped up the volume and leaned forward on the couch.

"The yellow patch on the south side of the hurricane shows an area that is weakening beyond what we've seen in a decade. We are approaching the slow down that seems to happen to Hurricane Goliath every ten years, and this weak spot has appeared earlier than it has in the past. Experts are hopeful this could be the signal that Goliath is finally going to hang up his hat and move on…"

I jumped up. "Did you hear that? It's weakening! Like, for real!"

Mella opened her mouth, then closed it. Even Trig stood frozen and silent. We stared at the screen as the meteorologist played the radar image over and over.

Mella grabbed my hand. "Don't get too excited, Ash. It could be nothing."

I yanked my hand away. "Or it could be something. I've never seen that before. The radar images have been one hundred percent consistent until that spot."

"I've seen it before." Mom walked in with a gaudy plastic crown and pink feather boa in her hand. "They're right; this happens every ten years, and it's happening two weeks earlier this time. You guys wouldn't remember it because you didn't care about this stuff back then."

I sat back down, confused by the look on Mom's face. This weakening was remarkable news, but she was blinking fast, and her voice shook. I activated the record function on the app in order to watch the report later and switched off the screen. It wasn't the best time, but I had to ask anyway.

"Ten years? So, like when Dad?"

Mom took a deep breath, then smiled at me, as if she had just noticed I was standing there. "Happy Birthday, Mini-Muffin." She draped the boa around my neck and plunked the crown on my head. "It's time for the birthday traditions."

Classic Mom. She was a master at ignoring a question she didn't want to answer and moving on to whatever inconsequential thing she could drum up.

Mella popped up wearing her I-Support-Mom face. "Let the Birthday Rituals commence!"

Fine. I guess my birthday was a good reason to change the subject.

I tossed the feather boa over my shoulder in true diva fashion and adjusted the crown on my head. "Okay. But where's Penn? We can't start anything without him."

Mom wiggled her eyebrows. "He's running an errand."

I burst out laughing. "You mean, he's picking up my chocolate chocolate chip bundt cake?"

Mom shrugged and widened her eyes. "Who knows what errands he runs on this random day in March?"

I flopped back on the couch. "Mom. We do the same things every year. I'm eighteen. I think you can stop pretending about these birthday surprises."

Trig snatched the crown off my head. "Yeah, and you can stop pretending like you don't know who the Tooth Fairy is either."

Mom grabbed the crown from Trig and gave him a motherly smack on the head. "Don't ruin it for the kids."

I giggled. "Yeah, especially since we haven't had a need for a tooth fairy in, what, seven years?"

Mom stuck out her lower lip. "Don't remind me. It's bad enough that my baby can now vote. I would rather spend today ignoring the fact that you guys don't need me anymore."

I jumped up and hugged Mom around the waist. "I'll always need you."

Penn burst through the door holding a white cake box up high, his hair flopping across his forehead. "Let the Birthday Rituals commence!"

Mella put her hands on her hips. "I already said that."

Penn lowered the box and frowned. "Without me?"

I took my place in the armchair and Mom handed me back the crown. "Don't worry, Penn. We haven't done anything except disparage the existence of the Tooth Fairy."

Penn humphed and tried to fix his hair back into whatever perfect style the fashion apps had convinced him of this week. "That's my favorite part."

Mella dashed out of the room and came back with plates, forks, and a knife. My family settled into seats, and Mom took the cake out of the box.

"Today, at four-oh-five pm--"

"So not for ten minutes," Trig said.

Mom silenced him with her patented Mom look. "This afternoon, at four-oh-five pm, Ashlyn will have been breathing on this earth for eighteen years. At this very moment on March sixth, eighteen years ago, your dad and a nurse named Beulah--"

"Beulah with an H," Mella said.

Mom nodded. "Beulah with an H was holding up my legs as I got ready to push."

I groaned. "At what age do we skip this part of the ritual?"

Mom went on like I hadn't spoken. Rude. "After one push, Ashlyn shot into the world, her path paved by her three siblings before her. At that moment, I loved those three other children more than anything, because they made the delivery of my fourth child the easiest delivery in the world. For that reason, on the anniversary of Ashlyn's birth, I award Mella, Trig, and Penn the very first slices of Ashlyn's birthday cake.

Trig hummed a triumphant tune while Mella cut three fat slices out of my birthday cake. I scowled as each of my siblings shoved big bites into their mouths and made obnoxious yummy sounds. But who was I to argue? It was all part of the ritual.

Mom snapped her fingers, and the yummy sounds stopped. "Ashlyn, since it is your birthday, you get to bestow the next piece of your birthday cake to whomever you choose."

My throat got tight, and I perched on the edge of the chair. This part was the worst. "I choose to bestow the next piece to Dad."

Mom nodded, her eyes bright with tears again. She leaned over and cut a small sliver of cake, placed it on a plate, and handed it to me. I took the plate and walked over to the mantle where our ten-year-old family picture stood. I pulled down my sleeve and wiped a layer of dust off the frame, then set the cake next to the picture. "Dad, here's your cake. You can come home anytime and eat it."

"But if you're not home by nine o'clock tonight, I'm going to eat it for you," Trig piped in. No one laughed at Trig's joke. Even though it was true. At nine that night, Trig would get that cake and take it to his room. I had the weather app to help me. He had a birthday cake five times a year to help him.

Mella cleared her throat. "And now for the ordering of dinner."

I turned around. "Ten bucks to whoever can order my birthday dinner for me, with one hundred percent accuracy."

Penn and Trig started talking at the same time. "Chicken lo mein from Hong Hing's Palace, with a double order of crab cheese wontons and" The order trailed off as they devolved into a wrestling match, each trying to cover the mouth of the other. Penn was bigger and stronger than Trig, but Trig played dirty, licking Penn every chance he got.

Mella laughed. "I wouldn't lick Penn if I were you. You don't know where he's been."

Penn grunted and pinned Trig to the couch. "Yeah. Try to guess when I showered.

I wrinkled my nose. "Ew. You guys were way off, anyway. Today is my birthday, not just any day. Could we get spaghetti from Blue Parrot?"

Mom put her arm around my waist and kissed my hair. "With meatballs or sausage?"

"At least one sausage. That was, I mean is, Dad's favorite. And I'll eat it."

Mom nodded, and Mella handed me the cake box with a fork. As the birthday girl, I got to eat the last half all by myself. I smiled at her and took a bite, letting the soft cake melt onto my tongue. Mella grabbed the boys by their arms and hauled them toward the kitchen, firing instructions about how to set up the table for my birthday dinner.

The quiet, empty room gave me time to think. I stared at my cake and sighed. We had long ago stopped putting candles on our birthday cakes and making birthday wishes. We always wished for the same thing: to find Dad.

CHAPTER 2

I GATHERED MY SCHOOL bag and the cake box, then headed to my room. Technically, I had some reading to do and a math assignment to complete, but it was my birthday. I'd skim through the English assignment later, and the calculus could wait until study hall in the morning. It would only take me five minutes anyway, since we had populated most of the answers on the math app in class. In ten weeks and two days, I would graduate from high school. That was the only math I needed to pay attention to. I had collected enough extra credit in most of my classes that I could flunk the rest of my assignments and still pass with middle marks in each class. Then again, I needed high marks to earn the scholarship for Eckman University.

Sighing, I pulled out my tablet to complete my homework. Might as well get it over with. The fragrance of chocolate called to me, though. The first time Dad had brought me a bundt cake was for my eighth birthday. He snuck it into my room after I had gone to bed, and we ate it with the lights out. I kept giggling, and he kept shushing me, warning that Mom might come in and break up the party. Or worse, that Trig and Penn might hear and come to eat all my cake. Apparently, that had been his birthday tradition with my sister and brothers, but it only started when we turned eight.

I opened the box and took another bite with the fork I had left inside, unsure of how the sweet dark chocolate would make it past the lump in my throat. A car door slammed. I jumped, then laughed a little. Sometimes I still felt like I was sneaking the cake in my room with my dad.

"Ashlyn! Your gentleman caller is here!" Trig called up the stairs in a high-pitched, bad English accent. He thought he was so hilarious.

I peeked out the window just as Mason climbed our last step. Butterflies kicked up in my stomach and I touched my hair. Had I fixed it well enough after Trig had ruined it? I whirled around and stared at my reflection in the mirror. Nope, I had not. I looked on my dresser for an elastic band, ready to toss it into a top knot. I hoped top knots would come back in style soon.

Mason had told me more than once that he liked my hair down. I ran my fingers through my long locks, trying to smooth out the craziest parts, then decided the wild look was the one I was going for, anyway. Besides, I was wasting time. Why spend another second on my dumb hair when I could spend it with him?

Mason and I had been unofficially official boyfriend/girlfriend since the start of our senior year. Mason's mom didn't believe that he should have a girlfriend while he was still in high school, but everyone knew we were together.

I forced myself to take normal steps down the stairs. I was eighteen now. An adult, not some flighty high schooler. I stopped when I heard voices in the kitchen.

"So, what's the status?" Mom said.

Mason's rich voice filled the hallway. "Nothing has changed. I mean, I'm moving forward like we talked about. I want you to understand that I still care about Ashlyn, and I promise to treat her with respect."

"I know you do." It sounded like Mom was smiling. "You're a dream partner for my little girl. And you kids are eighteen now. I would appreciate it if you would keep me in the loop about your plans, but ultimately, I have no control over your actions. And I don't want to stop you either. I trust you both, and simply ask for the courtesy of being informed."

My breath caught. I bounced between elation over what I heard and guilt that I had eavesdropped. I'd had a crush on Mason since our freshman year. It took until our junior year for me to realize he liked me back. It felt unreal that he stood in my kitchen, expressing his love for me to my mom.

I needed to get in there, but I paused for one extra second to inhale the amazing scent of Mason's cologne. I loved the fresh smell that permeated whatever area he was in.

"Are you spying?" a voice hissed in my ear. My face flamed as I whirled around and scowled at Trig.

"Shh," I whispered.

"Pee-yew! Mason, did you forget to shower today?" Trig gave a loud cough and brushed by me, waving his hand in front of his nose.

I heaved out a sigh, the magical moment broken, and rushed into the kitchen. "Don't laugh or answer that. If we ignore him, he'll learn that no one appreciates that kind of behavior, and he'll choose different interactions. Right, Mom?

Mom nodded and smiled. "That's right. He's looking for negative attention, and the way to stop it is to respond only with positive attention to positive situations."

Trig folded his arms and flopped into a chair. "It's rude to psychoanalyze someone if he is in the room."

I turned away, afraid he'd see my grin and undo all my hard work. Mom could deal with him.

Mason gave me a soft smile that showed his dimples. It was the kind of look that made me wonder if he noticed that there were other people in the room. Like the old stories say, my knees went weak. However, I was aware that there were other people in the room. I moved closer to him and tried to give off a nonchalant vibe.

"Hey."

"Hi."

"Ooo, such a romantic conversation!" Trig's high, annoying English accent was back. I tore my gaze from Mason to glare at Trig. Forget everything I ever said about him being my favorite.

Mom stepped in between us. "Okay. Ashlyn, why don't you and Mason step outside? But please don't leave. We'll eat as soon as Mella gets back with the food. Mason, are you going to stay?"

Mason shook his head. "No, Mom didn't want me staying out because I haven't finished my homework. I wanted to see Ash because I didn't see her after school."

Trig made kissy sounds, and Mom nodded. "Well, it's up to you. You're always welcome."

Mason smiled a charming grin, then turned to me and nodded his head toward the door. I turned to Mom with pleading eyes.

She laughed. "Yes, I'll keep Trig in here. He needs to sit in the Time-Out chair for a while."

"Thanks, Mrs. Booker."

"I told you. Call me Livvy."

"Right. Livvy." Mason looked uncomfortable, but smiled. He and I scooted out the door, where he grabbed my hand and pulled me to his car. He had parked in our favorite spot—on the street next to the lilac bush. The tall branches stood tall and empty, but they gave us some privacy. No one could see us from the front door. And I didn't care about anyone else in the cul-de-sac.

"Happy Birthday, Love."

I smiled and laced my fingers through his. "You already said that. Remember? After study hall? And at lunch? And twice at my locker?"

"But I didn't give you a present." Mason reached into his car and pulled out a brown paper bag. "Um, sorry it's not wrapped very well. Mom didn't have any wrapping paper, and I didn't want to ask her to get some, because she'd know I bought you a present."

I took the wrinkled bag and grinned. "And you couldn't buy some yourself?"

His dimples stained pink. "Um, where do you get that stuff? Is there like a special store or--?"

I laughed and squeezed his bicep, the solid muscle tensing beneath my fingers. "I'm teasing you, silly. I know guys don't care about things like wrapping paper."

"Yeah, but where do you get it?"

"The same place you get birthday cards."

Mason's face paled. "I didn't get you one of those. I can leave now and be back in ten minutes.

I set the bag on the hood of his car and clutched both of his arms. "Hey, don't worry about it. Seriously." I stood on my tiptoes and gave him a quick peck on the lips. Mason caught me around the waist and pulled me close. I placed my hands on his chest and bit my lip. Why did I suddenly kiss him like that? We had only had our first kiss two weeks ago. Me planting one on him like that was something couples who had been kissing forever did. I just didn't want him to feel bad about the birthday card, and then...

And then Mason was kissing me. For real. Until now, we had only been giving each other brief and light kisses, mostly because neither of us had any prior experience with kissing and we weren't sure what to do. But this kiss was different. He was gentle, but purposeful. For a second, I considered pulling away in case Trig was spying, but then all I could think about was how amazing kissing was. Why had we waited so long to kiss? Oh yeah, his mom.

The thought of his mom killed the mood a bit, and I pulled away, my cheeks on fire. "Didn't you bring me a present?"

Mason shook the dazed look from his face. "Oh yeah! Open it. I hope you like it."

I reached for the bag, my heart racing. A gift from my boyfriend on my birthday was one of those top ten special moments, and I didn't want to rush it. But I also wanted to see what he got me.

My heart dropped. "A pizza cutter?" Oh no. Mason was a lame gift-giver.

Mason nodded, beaming. "It represents the real gift. I signed us up for a pizza-making class at Matteo's. And it's in three weeks. I hope that's okay."

That pesky, moody heart of mine kick-started its happy dance again. "Oh my word. This is amazing. How did you think of it?"

He looked at his feet. "Um, Dasha helped me. She said you've always wanted to do cooking classes."

Dasha. My amazing BFF. I made a mental note to text her a thank-you message. I laid the pizza cutter on the hood of the car and threw my arms around Mason's neck, my lips seeking his. This time I took charge, letting him know how much I loved him too. He settled his hands on my hips and kissed me back, and I forgot everything—where we were standing, what day it was, that he had an over-protective mom, that there was a hurricane and that my dad...

"Ahem."

I jumped back, the magical bubble popped for the second time that day. Was this what being in a relationship was like? Getting interrupted all the time?

"Careful kids. You don't want to turn into a teenage cliche, do you?" Chip Sinclair, my mom's boss, stood at the end of our driveway with his arms folded, an amused grin stretching his mouth.

I pressed my hand to my burning cheek. "Uh"

Mason grabbed my hand and pulled me close again. "I don't mind, if it means I can kiss her."

Chip's laughter boomed, echoing in our quiet cul-de-sac. I cringed. Just what I needed, someone drawing attention to us. "Yeah, enjoy it while you can. You can get away with your free expressions of love at your age. If you ever get to my age and find yourself in love, you'll realize it's not quite as appropriate to make out on the street."

Mason laughed and squeezed my hand. I tried to laugh too, but it came out as a pathetic squeak. "What are you doing here?"

"Birthday dinner. Chinese, right?"

My mouth dropped open. "You're here for my birthday dinner?"

"Your mom invited me. I brought a gift." He said it as if the birthday gift was his automatic ticket to a public event. Our family had known Chip since before I was born, but we had never, like, hung out with him. He was just my mom's boss. Him standing on my driveway in khakis and a polo shirt, with no tie, was the weirdest thing I'd seen.

"Oh, um. Okay. But we're not having Chinese. We're having Blue Parrot. It's spaghetti and--"

"I love the Blue Parrot." Chip jammed his hands in the pockets of his khakis. "It was your dad's favorite place. We used to go there on Friday nights in college with your mom. If we got there right before closing, and they'd give us the stuff they didn't sell. You know, the leftovers that they were supposed to throw out at the end of the night. We lived on cold spaghetti most weekends."

"Why didn't you just warm it up?" Mason folded his arms and leaned against his car, his eyes twinkling. He looked ready to settle in for a witty bantering session with Chip. What was going on here?

Chip shrugged. "It was right when the government outlawed microwaves and introduced the flash cooker. We didn't know how to use it, so we ate most things cold. Anyway. Looking forward to the spaghetti. See you inside, Ash."

Ash. Why was he calling me Ash? Only my friends and family called me Ash. I would not put Chip Sinclair in that category.

Mason grabbed my hand and twirled me around to face him. "Hey. It'll be fine. I'll message you later, okay?"

I nodded, and Mason bent down to give me a soft kiss. I grabbed my pizza cutter and used it to wave goodbye as he climbed into his car.

He rolled down his window and leaned out. "Hey, Ash. I love you."

I grinned as he drove away. "I love you, too!" My shout shattered the quiet of the cul-de-sac, but this time I didn't care.

CHAPTER 3

THE EUPHORIA OF MASON'S present and kisses wore off three seconds after I walked back into the house, the magical bubble popped by a deep chuckle coming from the kitchen. I peeked in and froze. Mom leaned against the counter while Chip reached over her head to pull down the stash of birthday paper plates we had collected over the years.

"No, I think it's great." He shuffled through the assortment, a plastic smile pasted on his face as he took in the unicorns mixed in with the old comic book characters. "Ooo, Spiderman. I loved him as a kid."

"So did Jonah. Which is why Penn was obsessed with him until he was fifteen."

"Fifteen?"

Mom turned on Mama Bear mode and snatched the plate from his hand. "Well, when Jonah went missing, Penn did everything he could to stay close to him. I'm not going to shame him for that."

Chip tucked a strand of hair behind Mom's ear. "Of course not, Livvy. I get it. Whatever you all need, I'm okay with."

My stomach rolled, and I tiptoed away. Something weird was going on in that kitchen, and I needed answers. Preferably before I had to share Dad's favorite spaghetti with Mom's boss.

I went up the stairs, stomping on the third and eighth stair to make the loudest creak possible. Maybe that would break up whatever was going on in the kitchen. Trig's bedroom door was closed, but I had to talk to him.

I gave three light knocks, then cracked the door open. "Trig?"

"Dude, go away!" His voice boomed out over the rustling of paper. "It's your birthday. Birthday rule number six—closed doors are off limits."

"I'll close my eyes, but I have to come in. Like, right now. I'm serious." My voice caught as my throat squeezed shut. This weirdness was making me emotional.

He huffed out a sigh. "Okay, okay. Sheesh. Birthday rule number two—no crying on your birthday."

I clapped my hand over my eyes and pushed my way into his room. The scent of body spray and stale popcorn helped me calm down. I needed something normal right then, and nothing was more normal than Trig's unwavering passion for popcorn.

"Okay. It's safe. Open your eyes and tell me why you're freaking out."

I dropped my hand and sat on his bed. "Chip Sinclair is in our kitchen."

"Uh, yeah. I let him in."

"But he's here for my birthday dinner. Like, he's going to eat it. With us."

He clasped his hands together and leaned forward. That movement also helped calm me down. As the peacemaker in our family, he had great listening skills. Whenever he looked me in the eye like that, I could tell his full focus was on me. "Don't worry, okay? He's a friend. He knew Dad. So he understands what we need to do."

"But on my birthday? That's weird, right?"

Trig twisted his mouth, then shrugged. "Yeah, it is. But it'll be okay. Maybe he even bought you a present."

I snorted. "It better be a good present. Not lotion. Why is lotion the go-to present for girls, anyway?"

"Because everyone knows that a teen girl's sole mission in life is to smell like fruit and flowers." Trig batted his eyes and pretended to fluff his hair.

I grabbed his pillow and tossed it at him. "At least that's better than smelling like stale popcorn. Ew, is that popcorn in your bed?" I brushed a few kernels onto the floor. Trig snatched them up and popped them in his mouth, which made me gag and laugh at the same time.

"Listen, Ash. Don't worry about Chip, okay? Mom needs friends too."

I folded my arms. "Yeah. It's just that we've never had friends at our birthday dinners before. And she didn't even give us a heads up."

"Hey, I need help with this food! Penn and Trig, get down here now!" Mella bellowed up the stairs.

Trig jumped up and saluted. "I've been beckoned."

I nodded. "You don't want to keep the General waiting."

He darted out the door, then poked his head back in the room. "No snooping in here. Get out."

I stalked out into the hallway. "The stench of popcorn was making me nauseous, anyway." I grinned as I followed him down the stairs. Dinner with Chip wouldn't be so bad, as long as Trig was there with me.

I stepped into the bustle of the kitchen and bit my lip to keep from laughing out loud. Chip had pressed himself in the corner, his eyes wide open as the chaos of my family swirled around him. Mella barked out orders. Penn took his time following them, which made Mella bark louder. Trig opened the takeout containers and sampled a bite out of each one.

Mom bumped Chip with her hip to move him away from the cabinet. "Here, you can help me. Put ice in all these glasses. Trig, if you're going to sneak bites, at least use a fork. And while you're at it, put forks on the table. Penn, we'd like to eat before Ashlyn turns 19, so get a move on. Ashlyn, please take your seat. Dinner is almost ready. Oh, and don't forget your crown."

The crown and feather boa used to be one of my favorite birthday rituals, but I felt silly with Chip there. But Mom loved it too, so I could suck up a little embarrassment. I draped the boa around my neck and sat at the table, just as the rest of my family finished up the dinner preparations. I drew in a deep sniff of the spicy marinara and closed my eyes, letting the smell take me back to the time when the sixth person at our table was Dad and not Chip.

Mom clinked her knife on her glass. "Let the Birthday Ritual commence." I reached for the bowl with the noodles, glad that I got to have the first serving. On Penn's birthday, the rest of us were lucky to get a bite of food, since most of it ended up on his plate.

I had really been looking forward to this meal. Not only did I get to choose the food, but my whole family was together. Well, my whole family minus Dad. All of us being in the same room became rare over the past year. Someone was always at work, and Mom came home way after dinner most days. But on birthdays, we all ate together no matter what.

At the end of the meal, Chip wiped his mouth on his napkin and leaned back. "So, is it time for birthday cake?" My siblings and I traded nervous looks. See, this was the problem with having a random person at a Booker family birthday.

Mom smiled. "No, in our family, we eat the birthday cake before dinner. Ash, can Chip have a piece?"

My mouth dropped open. "But it's in my room."

"Is it possible for you to walk upstairs and get it?"

My heart pounded. I admit I was being a brat, but this was my cake. We had already done the ritual.

Chip reached over and grabbed Mom's hand. "Liv, don't make her go. I don't need cake. I'll go with whatever your family usually does. I want to be involved, not take over, remember?"

Wait a second. Why were they holding hands?

Mella narrowed her eyes. "What do you mean, 'be involved?"

Mom leaned back and gave a nervous laugh. "Well, okay. Since dinner is done, now is as good a time as any. Um, kids, I guess I should tell you that Chip has asked me if we could start dating and, well, I said yes."

Trig blinked. "Dating who?"

Chip scooted closer to Mom's and put his arm across the back of her chair. "Dating her. Dating each other. Look, I'll be honest, you're all adults now. I hope to marry your mom, and take care of her for the rest of her life. And of course, that means I'm here to take care of you, too. I mean it, whatever you need, you can come to me." He locked eyes with Mom, and she blushed, a radiant smile dancing across her lips.

The spaghetti, sausage, and chocolate cake threatened to come up. I jumped, knocking over my chair. "You're getting married?"

Mom shook her head. "Oh sweetie, no. I mean, I would never date someone unless that was a possibility, but we don't have plans. I mean, we're not engaged or anything."

My head grew light, and I gripped. "Well, that's great, since it would be so hard to explain to Dad why you were engaged to someone else. Aren't there laws against being married to two people?"

"Ashlyn, sit." Mella pointed at my seat.

"I'm not your dog." I turned and ran upstairs, slamming my bedroom door extra hard. It was a childish move, but this was a disaster. Mom was dating Chip? Like, dating him the way I was dating Mason? Did they kiss? I regretted my choice of birthday dinner. The garlic taste in my mouth made me want to throw up. Heat flared from my gut to the top of my head. Blue Parrot was ruined. I could never eat it again, now that Chip had ruined the taste by linking it with his announcement that he wanted to marry my mom. Ugh, why wasn't he already married to someone else? Was something wrong with him? Mom should take that into consideration.

A light tap interrupted my pacing, and I flopped on my bed, burying my head under my pillows. "Go away."

"That's not a good idea."

I growled. "Mella, I mean it. Leave. I don't want to hear your lecture right now."

The bed shifted as she sat down. "Come on, Baby Sister. I'm not going to lecture you. But we need to talk this out."

I moved the pillow off my head and glared. "How can you be okay with this?"

Mella's face softened, and she rubbed my back the way Mom used to when I was little. "Because Mom needs someone. And Chip is, well, competent."

I let out a hard laugh. "Competent? Yeah, like that's a good reason to be in a relationship with someone."

"You've been reading too many romance stories. It's a perfectly good reason. And he's not terrible to look at. And he and Mom have history, so she won't have to explain everything to him."

I sat up, scattering the pillows on the floor. "You mean explain she doesn't know where her husband is? That he actually might, in fact, still be alive? Yeah, I can see how that would ruin a new love."

Mella moved over to put her arm around me. "Ashlyn, it's been ten years. Ten. If Dad were still alive, he'd be here, don't you think that?"

The heat of anger switched to cold fear. "He's not dead."

"No one ever comes back from Hurricane Goliath. You know that. No living thing can survive those winds. I mean, you've studied the hurricane more than any normal kid should, so I know you understand how this works."

I choked back a sob. "But he has to come home."

Mella laid her head on mine. "Oh, Sweetie. Dad was aware of the dangers when he agreed to go on the mission. He knew the risks, but thought his theory would help the rest of the country. It's time to accept it. He died doing something he believed in. We can still celebrate him for that, right?"

I sniffed. Was it really time to let him go?

"Now Mom can experience love and companionship again. We need to support her, because we're all moving on with our lives. She needs to be allowed to have one of her own. If she thinks that she'll be happy with Chip, then I'm all for it."

I wiped my eyes and stared out the dark window. "But what if Dad came back? I mean, what if?"

Mella huffed and stood up. "Jeez, Ash. You are so stubborn. Get over it. He's not coming back." She stalked out of my room, slamming the door behind her. I didn't even care. I wanted to think about Dad.

I was only eight when he left. He had a theory that needed testing, but he didn't want to burden anyone else with the risk of entering the storm. So he did it himself. He made it twenty miles in before all communication was cut off. The United States Hurricane Agency did everything they could, but they couldn't even find a trace of his trail. They had no idea if he stayed on course or got blown off somewhere. They monitored his projected path for months before declaring him lost. MIA. Missing in action, as if he were some military hero.

The sorrow of the moment when the men from USHA came to tell us they were ceasing all search and rescue operations had never gone away. I still don't understand why the agency didn't do more. And that's why the thought of Chip dating my mom made me want to throw up.

Chip Sinclair was the man in charge of the United States Hurricane Agency.

Chapter 4

"Spill it."

I jumped at the sound of Dasha's voice, almost falling off the stool attached to the round cafeteria table. My cheeks burned at the burst of laughter that followed my less-than-graceful gymnastic act. I scowled. I had been friends with Dasha, Rosalie, and Gretchen since sixth grade. Mason brought Jude and Zed to the group when he and I started eating together all the time. Lunch was usually one of my favorite parts of the day, when we'd all meet up. At least, it was until now, when they all looked at me like an unwilling participant in a viral video. My birthday was yesterday, but maybe I could get myself a new friend group as a late birthday gift to myself.

I picked at the lettuce peeking out of my chicken wrap. "Spill what, my drink? I'm surprised I didn't. Why are you all sneaking up to the table, by the way?"

Rosalie tossed her purple-streaked hair and grinned, her almond-shaped eyes twinkling. "Uh, we didn't sneak. We clomped toward you like a herd of elephants. You were just so busy looking like you wanted to murder that wrap that you didn't hear us."

Gretchen giggled. "Seriously, Ash. You looked scary."

Dasha snapped her fingers and glared at the group. "Hey. It's her birthday, and she'll cry if she wants to."

I couldn't stop the smile. My BFF Dasha. She was always in my corner, no matter what. "My birthday is over. Only little kids get birthday months."

Gretchen stuck out her lower lip. "Well, that's sad. I think I'll cry with you."

Dasha bumped my shoulder. "Come on. What's going on? You've usually inhaled half of your lunch before we even get here."

"Yeah, so you can spend as much time as possible holding hands with Mason." Jude batted his eyes and made kissy sounds, causing Zed to choke on his sparkling water.

Rosalie tossed her napkin at Jude. "Shut up. We actually want to hear what's wrong."

Mason plopped his lunch down and sat on the stool next to mine. "What's wrong with what?" My heart lifted and my shoulders relaxed.

I reached for his hand. "What's wrong with me."

"You haven't told them yet?"

Dasha huffed out a sigh. "If you all stop butting in, she can tell us."

The group laughed again, and I joined in this time. Dasha had the best way of lightening the mood.

"Well, last night was my birthday dinner--"

"Yeah, Chinese food," Zed cut in.

I sighed. "No, Blue Parrot. I'm not that predictable."

Gretchen cracked up. "Yes, you are."

"Listen, okay? Last night was my birthday dinner, and," I sighed, "my mom's boss ate with us."

The group had no words this time. No jokes, no comments. Just open mouths and blank looks.

"That guy in charge of USHA?" asked Jude.

I nodded, a lump growing in my throat. "Yeah. Chip Sinclair. It was totally weird. I mean, he's been around my family since before any of us kids were born. Like, he was friends with my parents in college or something. But then he and Mom dropped a bombshell."

"They found your dad?" Rosalie shrieked so loud that the normal din of the cafeteria came to a halt. Mason tightened the grip on my hand as my stomach did the roller coaster thing it always did when someone mentioned my dad. Just saying "found" and "dad" together made my hopes soar.

"No. He's dating my mom." Saying it out loud made me lose my appetite. I pushed my food away.

Dasha clutched my arm. "What? What does that mean?"

"Well, when two people like each other in a way that's more than friends, and they want to get to know each other, they spend time together in a way that's called 'dating.'" Zed laughed at his own joke. No one laughed with him, and Jude punched him in the shoulder.

I swallowed hard. "Zed is kind of right. I mean, they are dating dating. Like, for real. Chip even said he wants to marry Mom."

"But what about your dad?" Dasha leaned in close.

A tear trickled down my cheek. "Well, he's not here to stop them, is he?"

For a few minutes, the table was silent. I stared at my hand woven together with Mason's. Would Mom and Chip hold hands this way? The thought made my skin crawl.

Rosalie clapped her hands together. "Okay, what you can't do is worry about this. Worrying never solves anything. But planning does. What's the plan to stop the wedding?"

"Just call and cancel everything your mom sets up. Or I'll do it. I can hack into her wedding planner app and find out all the vendors she sets up." Gretchen pulled out her com like she was going to make calls right then.

Dasha placed her hand over the com. "Whoa, Gretch. That was super specific. And you thought of that idea quickly. Um, have you done this before?"

Gretchen rolled her eyes. "Come on, don't any of you watch movies anymore? I saw it in that movie that uploaded last week. The one with Ryker Hunt and Chloe Reid?"

"I love Ryker Hunt. He's so hot," Rosalie said.

I burst out laughing and everyone stared at me like I had lost my mind. Mason rubbed my back as I tried to catch my breath. "Oh my word. You guys are awesome. Like, you're the best friends ever."

Gretchen pursed her lips together. "So, do you want me to hack?"

I grinned. "There's nothing to hack. They aren't engaged yet. And the whole 'stop the wedding' thing is an overdone story, anyway. I won't do that."

She sighed and slid her com back into her cross-body bag. "Fine. But I'll do it if I have to."

"What movie was it again?" Rosalie mumbled around a bite of the meal replacement bar in her mouth.

"Gross, Rose. Manners." Zed wrinkled his nose. Rosalie showed Zed the chewed up food in her mouth and everyone laughed. The conversation moved to Zed's lack of manners and I grinned, my heart light. I needed this. A normal day with my normal people acting normal. Even the low racket of the crowd in the cafeteria and the smells of today's meatloaf and pizza were making me feel better. I jumped a little when Mason squeezed my knee, then laced my fingers through his once again. He pushed a cup of chocolate pudding toward me and my pulse raced. I glanced around to see if anyone noticed my cheeks growing warm, but everyone was wrapped up in a discussion about the movie that had given Gretchen sabotage ideas. Chocolate pudding was kind of a thing with Mason and me. Our first kiss had been after we shared a cup of chocolate pudding. Everyone's first kiss should be after chocolate pudding.

Mason leaned in to whisper. "I think I left my sweatshirt in the hall by tech storage. We should go get it when you're done with the pudding."

"You mean the hall where no one goes except the janitor?" I ripped open the lid and scooped out a bite.

Mason shrugged, grabbed the spoon, and took his own bite out of the cup. "Yeah. Weird, right?"

"So weird." I bit my lip to keep from smiling like a fool as Mason finished the pudding and gathered my lunch trash. He took it to the waste converter as I picked up my shoulder bag. Our friends were still teasing Rosalie about her love of Ryker Hunt and didn't seem to notice us leave. I was glad, because there were only seven minutes left in the lunch period, and I didn't want to spend them trying to ditch my friends. Not when Mason had the fresh taste of chocolate pudding on his lips.

That moment with Mason in the abandoned hall by tech storage carried me through the rest of the day. I sailed through my homework as I pictured me and him at Eckman University in the fall, finding our own secret spot on campus to sneak a few minutes together between classes. The big stone sculptures at the edge of the courtyard seemed like a good idea. Although that was too obvious. There might be a bench somewhere near the dorms—

"Ash, dinner." Mella opened the door to my room, breaking into my beautiful daydreams.

I scowled. "Ever knock?"

Her eyebrows shot up. "I did. You said come in."

My face heated. "I did?"

She looked amused. "Senioritis. Hang in there, girl. You still have three months to go."

"Ten weeks and one day."

"Whatever. Come on."

I hurried down after her and slipped into my chair. Mom and Trig were already sitting. Penn lumbered in and sat down too, and my mouth dropped open. Our whole family eating together two days in a row? It was some kind of birthday miracle. We spent the next few minutes in the circus that is passing around food in my family, then Mom clinked her knife on her glass.

"Attention. I call this meeting to order."

My heart pounded, drumming out the happy thoughts of a fun family meal. "Meeting? What meeting?"

Mom shrugged. "I figured we were having a meeting since we're all eating together again."

I glanced around at my siblings. They exchanged looks and nods, arguing silently. I froze. That was new.

Mom laughed. "Come on, out with it. Is this about Chip? Because it can be. We should have a conversation about that."

Mella shook her head. "Well, sort of. I mean, we don't need to talk about Chip. We're happy for you, Mom. But since Chip is now in the picture, we--"

"Me and Mella and Trig," Penn jumped in.

Mella scowled. "We were thinking we would—"

Trig punched Penn in the shoulder. "But not together. I mean, me and Penn, together."

Mella glared at the boys. "Stop with the interrupting."

Sometimes the banter between my brothers and sister made me laugh. This was not one of those times. "What are you talking about? Just say it." Everyone stared at me. I guess my voice had been louder than I thought.

Trig sat up straight. "We're moving out."

"Smooth." Mella huffed out an exasperated sigh. "Since Mom has Chip and Ashlyn goes to college in the fall, we think it's time for us to move on as well. I mean, that way, Mom and Chip can spend time as a couple, and Ashlyn doesn't need our help."

"Me and Penn found an apartment in Castle Pines. It's only ten minutes away, Ma, so we'll still be close." Trig puffed out his chest like this was an amazing feat.

"And I'm going to move in with Amara. Her roommate is moving out, and she needs someone to share the rent." Mella fiddled with her napkin, her eyes never leaving Mom's face.

The kitchen went silent. I stared at Trig as I tried to replay his words in my head.

"Wait, what?" My voice squeaked, but there was nothing I could do about it.

Trig laughed. "Put down the fork, Ash. You don't need to stab anyone right now."

I put down the fork I didn't even know I had picked up. "What did you say?"

Mom had tears in her eyes and she gave me a soft smile. "They're moving out, sweetie. As they should. They're twenty-three, twenty-one, and nineteen. I never expected them to live at home forever." She reached over to smooth out Penn's hair. "I know you all have stayed longer than you should have just to help me out, and I love you for it. But of course you should move on. Your dad and I always knew you would fly the coop someday, and we were so excited to see each of your journeys unfold. Well, I'm so proud. And I can't wait to see your new apartments."

I pushed away my plate. "So just like that? You're all moving out and moving on? Perfect. Guess I missed the part where family is only family until some get bored and decide to leave."

Mella gave me the look that always ticked me off the most: the Poor Wittle Ashlyn look. "Ash, you're moving out in the fall."

I folded my arms. "Yeah, to college. And only if I get accepted. But in case you didn't know, I won't live at college permanently. I get to come home for weekends and breaks and summers."

Trig clasped his hands together and leaned toward me. How did that movement always soothe me? It was so condescending. "It's going to be okay. We're only ten minutes away, and we'll come back to do laundry."

I snorted. "So, like, once a month? Because that's how often you guys wash your stinky clothes."

Mom sighed. "In a normal family, they would have moved out one by one, as they got older. But we've never been a normal family, have we? I know it's hard to have them all go at once, but we'll manage. Mella, how far is it to Amara's place?"

"She's in Lone Tree, so just 20 minutes." Mella straightened. "How about we do family dinner night? Whatever day you want. Except Thursdays. I work late on Thursdays."

"Not Mondays, either. Monday Night Football and all." Trig shoved a bite in his mouth.

"And Chip has executive meetings on Wednesdays." Mom tucked her hair behind her ear and took a sip of water, as if throwing in Chip's schedule to our family plans was a common occurrence.

My siblings all launched into talking at once about their new places and their new schedules. Mom was right. If Dad had been here, then Mella, Trig, and Penn would have all moved out one by one, as soon as they graduated from high school. Mella would have gone to college to be a nurse instead of stopping with her CNA license. Trig would have gone to school for psychology. Penn might have worked at the auto shop and moved in with friends sooner.

The problem was, if they were all moving out, then it meant that no one wanted to wait at home for Dad. I had just assumed that when I went to college, my siblings would be here the minute Dad got back. But no one would be here. Except Mom. And Chip.

I shoved a few bites into my mouth and moved around the rest of my food so Mom wouldn't worry about me eating. Then I mumbled something about homework and fled to my room. It was time I got used to the fact that no one in my family believed Dad was coming back.

Chapter 5

Three things should have made me happy: it was Friday, the new shirt that Mella gave me for my birthday, and the thought of seeing Mason in less than two hours. But I couldn't muster up joy about any of them. Well, I had a little joy about the shirt. I looked amazing in the blue, scoop-necked tee.

I heaved a sigh and plopped down at the kitchen table to eat some yogurt. I wasn't hungry for breakfast, but I had a test in AP Natural Science, and I didn't want to have a blood sugar crash or anything.

"Morning, Sunshine." Mom breezed in and sailed over to the coffee panel. She put her travel mug in the opening and pressed her thumb on the reader. AI confirmed her coffee order, replacing the stale odor of leftover spaghetti with the fresh scent of nutty chocolate brew. She hummed as she dug in the fridge, then turned around. Her smile vanished with one glance at me, and she hurried over to the table and sat. "Honey, what's wrong?"

I squirmed, wishing I knew how to keep my feelings off of my face. I should have eaten my yogurt in my room. "Nothing. I'll be fine."

Mom rubbed my arm. "Look, Ash. Changes are hard. But you're ready for this. All of it. You're ready to move on to college, and you're even ready for your siblings to move out. I know you like having them here, but you can handle things on your own. I've seen you do it, especially on the days where we all have to work. You do an amazing job of taking care of us, so you don't need us to take care of you. This next phase is going to be so fun. It will be about all of us learning about each other as adults and developing the kind of friendship that adult family members have. Less of me bossing everyone around, and more of us just enjoying each other's company when we get together."

I growled. Leave it to Mom to make everything sound wonderful, forgetting the worst parts. "Yeah, that all sounds great. But the truth is, we have no idea where Dad is. I'd support you moving on if we had proof that he died. But if he's alive, shouldn't we wait a bit more?" I clutched my yogurt cup tighter and traced the outline of the peach on the label. Dad loved peach yogurt the best.

Mom scooted her chair closer and put her arm around my shoulders. "I will always love your dad. He was my first true, real, honest love. The first person who showed me love went beyond butterflies and kissing. He gave me the greatest gifts on the planet—you and your sister and brothers. And I loved him enough to let him do what he was passionate about. He was so invested in that hurricane. We both understood the risks of his mission, and I knew he would never forgive himself if he didn't try to gather the data he needed. He would never have asked anyone else to go in for him. But honey, it's been ten years. Our hearts were connected at the core, and I firmly believe he is no longer with us. If I felt a glimmer of hope, of course I would wait. But my spirit knows that my soul mate is gone. I've known for a long time, but I wanted to make sure you kids were ready for your own lives before rebuilding mine."

The yogurt soured on my tongue. "So it's our fault you've been alone for ten years."

Mom pressed her lips together. "Don't twist my words. I'm saying that I've given it enough time. This whole thing with Chip is new for me too. It's strange to imagine him as more than just a lifelong friend. But he's so confident and caring that my heart sparked when I finally let it. He's been wooing me."

I swallowed hard. I wasn't sure if I wanted the details. "Could you tell me the story later?"

Mom stroked my hair, then kissed me on my temple. "Of course, baby. Chip and I are going to take this very slow. If you truly can't come around to the idea of me being with him, I promise I will call it off. I will never put him over you or any of my kids. But I want you to promise to give it an honest chance, okay?"

My breath caught at the sadness in Mom's eyes. She really did like Chip. When Mason and I first became whatever we were, I had worried all the time that my family wouldn't like him. And Mrs. Wood's disapproval of our dating hurt. I never wanted Mom to feel that kind of hurt.

I nodded and wrapped my arms around her waist. "I promise. I'll give him a shot."

She smiled and looked at her watch. "Oh my goodness, I have to fly. See you tonight." She grabbed her coffee and hustled out the door. I sat and finished my breakfast, trying my best to think of all the good things about Chip. Part of the problem was I didn't know him that well. I didn't want to make room in my busy schedule to change that, but if it would make Mom happy, maybe I should.

I took my empty yogurt cup to the waste converter. Mom's lunch bag sat on the counter. Nuts, that was my fault. I glanced at my com. I had time to take her lunch to her and make it to school before the first bell rang, so I rushed to grab my things and headed out the door.

The quickest way to go to Mom's job and get back to school was by using mass transit. In the past, Grandma told us that using your own car was quicker, but that all changed with the completion of the light rail system in Denver. Now, no one could beat skipping stoplights or the trains' under-30-second stops. It was hard to believe the trip from our neighborhood's station to the USHA headquarters on the north side of Colorado Springs took Grandma an hour, when it only took us five minutes.

Thankfully, the line at security to get into the building wasn't too long. Just three people waited for the metal detectors. And Cody was on duty. Cody was, like, a million years old and had been a guard at USHA since before I was born. He was still young looking, thanks to skincare technology, but he let his hair go white to show off his age. He told me he did that to "throw the nefarious off their game." More than once, some jerk underestimated him because they thought he was too old to chase after him, but he was still fast and strong and chased down the people who tried to skip the security system without losing his breath.

Cody's eyes twinkled when I stepped up to the scanner. "Hello, Miss Ash. Happy birthday a few days late."

I grinned. "Thank you. Ugh, I forgot to bring you coffee."

He chuckled. "Well, I forgot to get you a birthday present, so we're even." He took my bag and Mom's lunch and swiped his handheld over the two, then waved me through the beam of light that scanned the rest of me. "Ah, good. May your skin always be as clear as your scans."

I laughed as I hurried away, wishing I had planned in a few extra minutes to chat with Cody, but I didn't want to be late for school. I took the tube up to Mom's floor and made it to her office without having to stop and talk to anyone else.

Harper, Mom's assistant, smiled as I walked up to her desk that sat next to Mom's door. "Ashlyn. So good to see you. You have off from school today?"

I held up Mom's lunch. "No, Mom left this. I had some time to bring it before my first class."

Harper tsked. "You're an amazing daughter. My daughter wouldn't even look at me her entire senior year of high school. And here you are, so helpful and polite. I wish you could have given my girl some Good Human lessons."

I laughed a little and inched toward Mom's office, trying to escape the awkwardness of being compared to Harper's daughter. "Well, I had the time, so--"

"She's not in. She was called to a meeting as soon as she got here, and I think it will last all morning."

"That's okay. I'll just leave it on her desk with a note." I put my hand on the door and waited for Harper to buzz me through. Harper smiled and waved, and I slipped inside. Mom kept a small pad of paper on her desk, even though that was an old-fashioned thing to do. Getting a paper note was more fun than a pop-up on her monitor. I scribbled out a little flower drawing and put her lunch next to her keypad, where she couldn't miss it, before moving back to the door.

A deep chuckle stopped me just before I stepped out into the hall. I peeked out to see Chip and another man walking toward Mom's office. I pushed the door, not fully closed but unlatched. My heart pounded. This could be a good time to begin building a bridge with Chip. I swallowed hard and gathered my courage. I could do this. I grabbed the door handle and took a deep breath.

"So, you and Livvy Booker?" I froze as they stopped outside Mom's office.

"Yeah. I've been after that prize for decades. Sometimes the four-hundredth time is the charm, am I right?"

"You mean you didn't give up after she got married?"

"Nah. I laid low for a long time, but as soon as Jonah was out of the picture, I turned back on my game."

"That was ten years ago."

"Patience, my friend."

"I hope she's worth it."

"Oh, she will be. I mean, in all these years, she's kept the same shape she had back in college. Only now she has the experience of a mature woman. I can't wait to handle that."

My stomach lurched and the peach yogurt threatened to come up.

"You haven't 'handled' that yet?"

"Watch it. She's a lady who waits until marriage, and I'm good with that."

I rolled my eyes. How chivalrous of him.

"Harper, where were you, and why is this open?" Chip's voice changed from joking to the bark of anger. The door slammed shut, and I jumped back, then pressed my ear against it.

Harper's reply came out muffled. "Well, her--"

"Ms. Booker's job is highly sensitive, and her door must remain closed and locked whenever she's not in there. I know for a fact that she is in a meeting until noon today. So if you want to keep your job, I suggest you follow protocol, no matter what. There is no excuse, do you understand?"

"Yes, sir."

Heat flared in my chest. Harper had been Mom's assistant for over seven years. She knew protocol. I waited by the door while Chip's voice moved down the hall. I pressed the button to open the door and peeked out. Harper looked at me with wide eyes and nodded. I stepped out and pulled the door closed behind me.

I twisted my mouth and gave her an apologetic look. "I'm so sorry. I should've closed the door behind me."

She shook her head. "No need for apologies."

"Mom would do anything to keep you here. So don't worry."

"I'm not. He threatens all of us assistants at least three times a week. You just get used to it. I'm not worried, honey, and you shouldn't worry either. Now, hustle to school. And go down that hall; Chip went the other way."

I mouthed the words "thank you," then hurried down the way Harper suggested, replaying Chip's words over and over. I'd never heard anyone talk about my mom like that. Sometimes I overheard guys in study hall talking about girls that way, but I always ignored it. What should I do with this information?

"You okay, Miss Ash?" Cody's voice snapped me out of my fog.

I nodded. "Yes, I'm fine. I just need to get to school."

"You're pale. You should go home and rest." He reached out and smoothed my hair the way my grandpa always did.

"No, I'm alright. Only ten more weeks until graduation." I forced my face to relax and smile.

"Okay, then. Have a good day and be safe."

"Thanks, Cody. Bye." I ran out the door to catch the light rail before it shot back to my end of town. For the first time, I wished those rides were longer. I needed time to think.

Chapter 6

I PULLED UP IN front of Dasha's house and engaged the parking system just seconds before she flew out her front door, her black, curly hair bouncing behind her.

"Ash!"

"Dash!" I fumbled with the button to open the door. "Argh, why won't this open?"

She cracked up, then leaned over to coach me on how to use a car. "Press the power button, silly. Why can't you remember to do that first?"

I growled and pressed the button to turn off the car. The door pushed opened with ease. "The car should know that if I've engaged the parking system, then I want to get out. These are supposed to be 'smart' cars. Well, this model needs to go back to school or something."

Dasha wrapped her arms around me, squishing my breath out. All the stress and worry about cars and Chip melted away in Dasha's famous hug.

"Your Friday community college classes cramp my style."

She grinned. "Yeah, but today was Textile Day."

I snatched my overnight bag from the backseat. "But I really needed to talk to you at school." Dasha grabbed my arm and pulled me behind her toward the house. "I have the worst news about Chip."

She stopped pulling me and turned to give me her full attention. "What?"

I glanced around and shook my head. "Not here. Inside."

She snorted. "Are you under surveillance or something? Is someone listening?"

"Just come on. It's going to be a long conversation, and I'm cold."

She looped her arm through mine. "I am so ready for a long conversation."

Her hug may have taken the edge off of my worry, but the aroma of Dasha's house made me feel lighter than I had before my birthday. It always smelled like cinnamon, and not the fake cinnamon either. A rich, spicy cinnamon that comes with the yummiest comfort food.

The Hart's house was my safe space. Mr. and Mrs. Hart were practically my second parents. Mr. Hart was even the one to teach me how to drive. I tried not to think about how many parts of my life Mr. Hart had filled that Dad had missed out on. Mostly because I wanted to be loyal to them both. I wished Dad had been with me all this time, but it made me sad to think that if Dad had been here, then I wouldn't have had Mr. Hart help with so many key points of my life.

Mr. Hart waited at the door as Dasha and I entered from outside. The wrinkles around his chocolate brown eyes deepened with his grin. "It's Ash and Dash." I couldn't stop the smile as he crushed me into a hug. Dasha had inherited her hugging skills from him.

"Hi, Mr. Hart."

He held me by my shoulders and dipped his head to look me eye to eye. "Ashlyn, you are now eighteen years old.

Considered an adult by the state of Colorado and our great nation. You can't buy alcohol yet, but you can vote. Which means it's time you called me Wyatt."

I stared at him for two seconds before bursting into laughter. "No way. Can't do it. You're Mr. Hart forever."

He dropped his hands and frowned. "But 'Mr. Hart' makes me feel old."

"Daddy, you are old. Embrace it." Dasha squeezed him around his waist.

The main floor of the house was a spacious room, connecting the kitchen, dining room, and family room. Everyone was always together, no matter what they were doing. Unlike my house, where every room was closed off into separate rooms.

Mrs. Hart waved us over to the kitchen. "Come on, y'all, let's eat."

I dropped my overnight bag in the entry way and took a deep breath, filling my soul with the scent of pot roast and gravy, laced with cinnamon. "Hi, Mrs. Hart."

She smiled at me. "Happy birthday, Sugar."

"Did you make a pot roast?"

"It's your birthday, isn't it?" She winked and pulled a bowl of Caesar salad from the fridge.

Julian, Dasha's sixteen-year-old brother, stomped through the great room and slumped into a chair at the table. "Oh sure. Ashlyn gets a pot roast. But when I want it, I'm stuck with freeze-dried pod meals."

I bit my lip. "I didn't make a special request or anything."

Dasha threw her arm around my shoulders and glared at her brother. "Stop grumping, Julian. It's her birthday. Plus, there is no need to complain when you get to eat the roast, too."

"Son." All Mr. Hart had to say was that one word.

"I'm joking. Happy birthday, Ash."

I smiled back, even as I studied his face. Julian annoyed Dasha most of the time, but I felt a special bond with him. We youngest kids had to stick together. It wasn't easy being the baby of the family.

Within a few minutes we had helped get the rest of the food on the table, and Mr. Hart had blessed the meal. I spooned the homemade mashed potatoes on my plate and gave a little squeal. "I love real mashed potatoes. I mean, the boxed ones my mom makes are great because they're done in five minutes, but you can't beat the real thing."

The Harts laughed, as they usually did, at my stories of eating at my house. I think they always thought I was joking. They didn't understand how my family had embraced convenience foods since Mom worked so much and they were easier for Mella to make.

"So, each of you tell me, what was the highlight of your day?" Putting down the gravy boat, Mr. Hart made eye contact with each of us in turn. This was my favorite part of eating with this family.

"I got to match textiles to paint samples." Dasha bounced like she had been holding in that tidbit all day.

Julian groaned. "He said highlight. Not 'most boring part of your day.'"

"Son."

Julian pasted a smile on his face. "I got an Exceeds Expectations on my essay on wind energy."

Mrs. Hart jumped up from her seat and ran around the table to grab him in a face-squishing hug. "Now that's my boy."

Dasha rolled her eyes. "You would think he didn't get Exceeds Expectations all the time. This is not a new thing."

Mrs. Hart kissed Julian on the head and sat back down. "So what? I'm proud of him each time it happens."

Mr. Hart twisted his mouth. "But we'd be proud of you, even if you weren't so strong in academics."

Julian smoothed down his shirt and picked up his fork. "Yeah, Dad. I know."

Mr. Hart nodded and turned to me. "And what about you, Ash?"

"Uh--" What to say? Chip's disgusting conversation about Mom had clouded my whole day. "This is the highlight."

Julian made a gagging sound, and Mrs. Hart smacked him with her napkin.

"I'm serious. It's awesome to be here. I love being a part of a whole family."

The table grew still as everyone stared at me with sad looks.

"Oh, Honey" Mrs. Hart reached over and grabbed my hand. My eyes filled with tears, and I blinked them away.

"Sorry. You said highlight, and I bummed you all out. I didn't mean to. I'm trying to say this is the best part and I'm so happy."

The silence at the table grew awkward until Julian shoved a bite of roast in his mouth. "Hey, did you all hear about the Storm Chaser rally?"

Mr. Hart shook his head. "I don't keep up with them."

I leaned forward at the word "storm." "Storm Chasers?"

Dasha gave me a funny look. "How is it possible that you've never heard of the Storm Chasers? They're fighting against USHA all the time. Hasn't your mom said anything?"

I shook my head. "She never talks about work. And, uh, I guess I don't ask."

"Don't worry, Honey." Mrs. Hart patted my arm. "My children don't ask about my work either. No one asked about my day, so none of them knew that the handhelds all frizzed out at the same time, so none of the reading testing got done in fourth grade."

Julian snorted. "And how is that your problem?"

"I'm the principal, honey. Everything in the school is my problem."

Dasha rolled her eyes. "Okay, okay. Ashlyn gets a pass, then. So the Storm Chasers are this group that has formed against USHA. They're always protesting something and getting on the news."

"They believe taxpayers' money shouldn't be spent on the storm when nothing can be done." Mr. Hart leaned back in his chair. "I understand where they're coming from, but I also know the great work your mom does at USHA."

I forgot about the plate of delicious food in front of me. "What do they do at the rallies?"

Julian kept shoveling his potatoes into his mouth. "I heard they're trying to raise awareness about the theory of the government using Hurricane Goliath's eye as a hidden jail. They can send anyone there and do anything they want to them because that spot on the globe is like a black hole."

I laughed. "No it's not. We have images from inside the eye."

"Do we? How do we know they are current, and not images taken from other storms? Or maybe they're using the same image from, like, forty-five years ago, because how would we know the difference?" Julian reached for the bowl of mashed potatoes and spooned another huge mountain of them on his plate.

Dasha reached over with her fork and scooped up a bite of potatoes from Julian's plate. "Sounds like you're interested in the rally, baby brother."

Julian slapped her fork with his. "No. But it's more interesting to talk about the Storm Chasers than any dumb school work."

Mr. Hart and Dasha laughed as Mrs. Hart launched into an impressive monologue about the joys of education while I picked at my food. I tried to listen, but all I could think about was the Storm Chasers. Why would they say the government had something going in the eye of the hurricane? Did they have evidence?

"You done?"

I snapped my head up. Dasha stared at me as the rest of her family cleared the table. Dinner was over. My face heated. "Oh, yeah. I'm done."

Dasha tugged on my arm. "Then come on. We've got a long conversation ahead of us."

My stomach sloshed the few bites of pot roast I had managed to get down. For that wonderful thirty-eight minutes, I had forgotten about the dark spot in my life called Chip Sinclair.

"Don't we have to help clean up?" Mrs. Hart always made me and Dasha help with dishes.

"Not on your birthday weekend, girl. Now get a move on before Mom forgets and ropes us into scrubbing something." Dasha slipped down the stairs to the basement with surprising stealth. I grabbed my overnight bag from the entry way and followed her with one last look at the kitchen. Mrs. Hart caught my eye and winked just as I headed down the stairs myself.

"What are you grinning about? Did Mason call?" Dasha had already set the mood in her walk-out basement bedroom. The glow from her fairy lights danced across her walls and the low sounds of the oldies crooned from her audio system. They should have never stopped making music like the Backstreet Boys. Boy bands rocked.

"No, your mom is just awesome. That's all." I tossed my bag in the corner, kicked off my shoes, and flopped on her queen-sized bed that was covered in way too many decorative pillows.

With a shrug, Dasha nestled on the bed's other side. "I guess. Now, Chip."

I groaned, took a deep breath, then launched into the whole story. I didn't leave out a single word.

Dasha sat still, her mouth hanging open. "Are you sure? For real?"

I nodded. "I wish I wasn't. I thought we had come a long way in respect for women. I've read stories about how men used to talk about women like they were objects to be used, but I thought we had evolved past it or something. And about my mom."

"What are you going to do?"

"Well, I have to tell Mom somehow, don't I?"

Dasha twisted her mouth. "Maybe you should wait and see. He could have been showing off for the person he was walking with."

My mouth was the one to drop open. "Are you serious? Are you saying it was okay for Chip to talk about 'handling' my mom just because another dude was there?"

"No, of course not. I'm just curious if it's a pattern, you know?"

I sighed. "I guess. But I still need to tell her. I just don't know how."

She shrugged. "We'll figure something out."

I plucked at a loose thread on her bedspread. "Sorry for such a bummer topic. See why I wanted to talk to you at school?"

"Speaking of school, let's talk about something fun. Like the senior trip."

I grinned. "We went a whole twelve hours without mentioning Seattle even once. That's our new record."

Dasha tossed a pillow at me. "Records are overrated. Now, I saw some cute booties today that we have to take on the trip."

"I don't want to buy boots. It's almost warm again."

"But we need boots if we're going to fit in at all the coffee shops. We need to look like we belong."

I tossed a pillow at her. "I like looking like a Colorado girl, thank you very much. Now, tell me more about the Storm Chasers."

She frowned. "Seattle talk is over already? But we haven't mapped out our coffee shop route."

"I'm pretty sure everything is already mapped out for us. It's a school trip, remember? We still have chaperons, and they'll tell us where to go and when to go there. How long have you known about the Storm Chasers?"

Dasha heaved out a giant sigh. "Fine. Five minutes of Storm Chasers, then back to Seattle. Deal?"

I held up my hand. "Promise. Okay, you know I feel like Dad is still alive. I can feel it in my soul. What if he's in the Eye? I mean, what if the Storm Chasers are right, and there are people held captive in there?"

"You think he's in jail in the eye?"

"I mean, he used to work at USHA with Mom and Chip. What if he crossed the wrong person, and they got rid of him by sending him to that jail?"

She bit her lip. "You make USHA sound like the mob or something."

I folded my arms. "After what I heard from Chip today, I wouldn't be surprised."

"I don't know, Ash. It seems like a stretch."

I traced the floral pattern on the bedspread. "Would you go with me to the rally?"

She winced. "That sounds like such a waste of time."

Tears threatened to spill from my eyes. Didn't she understand how badly I needed to do this? But it wasn't the right time to push her. I swallowed hard and put a smile on my face. "Okay, five minutes are up. Back to Seattle."

Dasha jumped off her bed. "Yes! Here, I mapped out a few possible routes on my tablet. Which do you think is best?"

I let her lead the conversation for the rest of the evening, but I couldn't forget about the Storm Chasers. I needed to talk to them.

CHAPTER 7

A VERY RUDE PERSON pounded on the door.

Dasha let out an animal-like growl and shoved her head under her pillow. "Julian go away." How could she be so loud, so early? My morning voice was always croaky.

"Darlin' Dash, it's me. It's time to get up." Mrs. Hart stepped into the room. I couldn't believe it. She was the rude person. "You have that lecture on color this morning, remember? And you asked me to wake you up at this very specific time?"

Dasha sat up, her hair sticking out to the side in an impressive swoop. "But I didn't ask you to pound on the door like my oaf of a brother."

Mrs. Hart rolled her eyes and pushed open the curtains, sunshine filling the room. "I tapped."

Dasha huffed and tumbled out from under the covers. "There has to be a nicer way to get up for something as awesome as a color lecture." She grabbed some clothes and shuffled off to the bathroom.

Mrs. Hart sat on the edge of the bed and patted my leg. "Ashlyn Honey, you can sleep in if you want. You can stay all day. Wyatt and I are taking Julian to his baseball tournament, so you'll have the house to yourself."

I yawned and thought for a minute. Spending the day in Hart's cozy house sounded very appealing. But I needed to do research on the Storm Chasers. I didn't want to do that on any of Dasha's devices. I kicked the warm, toasty blanket off my legs and sat up. "No thanks. I'll go home. I need to work on a project, anyway."

"Shower first? Or breakfast?"

I smiled and leaned over to give her a hug. "No, that's okay. But thanks, Momma."

She laid her head on mine. "I'll always be your second momma. You know that, right?"

"I know." A lump formed in my throat. "And I'll always be the twin daughter you never had."

With a kiss on my hair, Mrs. Hart popped up. "I'll let you get going. Don't forget to check your com for the coffee credit I just added, since I knew you'd leave. Order the fanciest drink you can come up with. It's your birthday, you know." She winked and slipped out the door, pulling it closed behind her.

I couldn't keep the smile off my face while I got dressed and threw my stuff back into my bag. I called out goodbye to Dasha through the bathroom door, even though she was singing too loud to hear me. The coffee from Mrs. Hart meant a five-minute detour, but the venti raspberry mocha with an extra shot of espresso made it worth it.

My house was silent when I got home, so I crept up the stairs, skipping the third and eighth steps. I wanted Mom to sleep as long as possible. Every moment she was asleep was a moment she wasn't with Chip.

I dropped my bag on my floor, sat on my bed, and sipped my coffee. I had a choice to make: lounge under the covers for a while and scroll through social media, or jump in the shower before my siblings took all the hot water? I glanced at my pillow, as if it would decide for me, when I saw the envelope.

My heart pounded in my ears. I slowly set the coffee on my nightstand. This was a life-changing moment for me. I closed my eyes and said a brief prayer before picking up the envelope with the unmistakable Eckman logo in the corner. It was larger than I had ever seen. Granted, I hadn't seen very many envelopes in my life. Almost all mail came through our coms or directly to our house screens. But for some reason, colleges still sent out these paper ones. Mom said it was because no one wanted to give up the thrill of receiving an acceptance letter by "snail mail," whatever that was.

I flipped the envelope over a few times, trying to figure out how to open it. I could see lines on the back, but no obvious opening. I growled and considered my options. Being an eighteen-year-old adult, I knew what was right. But I was still in high school; I could act a little foolish, right?

I tiptoed to Mom's room and lightly knocked on the door. She didn't answer, so I pushed it open and peeked in. She had buried herself under her covers as if she planned to sleep for a year. I decided she would want to be a part of this and went inside. My brothers and I had an old trick to wake Mom without getting in trouble. I wondered if it still worked. I moved over to her bed, knelt down, and rested my chin on the edge of the mattress, inches away from her face. And then I waited.

Mom drew in a sharp breath through her nose and her eyes popped open. Bingo.

She scowled at me. "Ashlyn, what are you doing? Why are you still as creepy as you were when you were a toddler?" She moaned and pulled a pillow over her head. "What time is it?"

"Um, it's only 8:15, and I am sorry to wake you, but I can't figure out how to get into this envelope, and I needed your help."

Mom popped into a sitting position, her eyes bright like she had been awake for hours. Her early morning movements surprised me. "Oh, I'm glad you woke me. No need for you to destroy anything important while trying to get into it. Quick, turn on a light or something."

I glanced at the Eckman logo, then handed over the envelope and opened the curtains. "Why didn't you teach me how to open envelopes as a kid?"

"So that you would always have to have my help to open up anything." Mom's grin was cheeky. "Now look; there's a small gap right here. You slide your finger in and gently tear. Make sure you aren't tearing any paper inside the envelope. And watch out for paper cuts."

I held my breath and did what she told me.

"Come on, Ash. Today. Don't go so slow."

"You said not to tear anything inside."

She pressed her lips together and folded her arms, the way she did when I was in kindergarten and wanted to put on my own shoes. I finally made it to the end of the envelope and saw another piece of paper inside. I swallowed hard and looked at her.

"Go ahead. Pull it out. Let's see what it says." Mom clutched her hands. I pulled out the paper and unfolded it, and cleared my throat to read out loud.

"Ashlyn Booker, congratulations on your acceptance at Eckman University for the upcoming fall term. Our continuing tradition of higher education" I got cut off as she threw her arms around my neck.

"You did it, Mini-Muffin. I knew you would, but knowing for sure makes me want to cry."

I let Mom hug me as I finished the letter. "It says I need to visit their site to find out the instructions for housing and to fill out the information for registration."

Mom wiped her face. "The envelope used to be thicker with information in the old days. But you have time. You can do that later. In fact, would you wait? I want to do that with you, but I need a shower and then I have to put in a few hours at the office."

I nodded. "I need to text Mason, anyway. If I got my letter, then I'm sure he got his."

A strange expression appeared on Mom's face. "Oh, sure. Okay, well, I'll be home by early afternoon. Maybe we can cook dinner together." Mom grabbed my hand as I stood to leave. "Ash, your future is wide open. Keep your options open too, okay?"

My heart sank. Those were not the words of celebration. "Are you saying I shouldn't go to Eckman?"

"No, of course not. I'm just saying that life doesn't always turn out like we plan, and I want you to hold your plans loosely, allowing for them to take shape in ways you never imagined."

"You're freaking me out, Ma."

Mom climbed out of bed and grabbed me in a hug. "I'm sorry. I'm not trying to. I'm thrilled you're going to Eckman. I just know you like to have things planned out, and I don't want any changes to steal your joy. Now, go text Mason. You have good news to share." With a swat on my backside, she headed for her bathroom and shut the door.

I took a deep breath. Mom must not have been fully awake. That was my fault. I should have let her sleep before opening the envelope. No matter. I had things to do. I snuck into Trig's room and picked up his com charging on the table next to his head. I slid his com under his thumb and pressed down, allowing the biometrics to unlock the device. I quickly typed a message, hit send, then waited five seconds before deleting it. Trig didn't move, even though I made a bit of noise putting his com back on the charging station. He always slept like the dead, which worked out well for me.

Code Lobster.

Mason's mom had a habit of monitoring his coms, so we had come up with the plan to use Trig's com to send secret messages when I needed to see him. Mrs. Woods would never let Mason leave to see me this early on a Saturday, but she'd probably laugh at the story he came up with to tell why Trig was sending him weird messages. He would know to meet me at our place in the park.

I don't remember getting ready or even driving. All I could picture was Mason and me studying together in the massive Eckman library, filled with honest-to-goodness books. We could hang out as often and as long as we wanted, without having to check in with Mom or Mrs. Woods. Then, the summer before our senior year, we'd get engaged. Since I would be almost done with my accounting classes, I could plan our wedding while Mason finished up with his pastoral ministries degree. Then we'd get married, and Mason would go to seminary, and we'd live in married student housing until he graduated. I pulled up to the park just as I pictured how I wanted our kitchen set up.

My heart skipped a beat. He was already sitting on our picnic table under the giant pine trees, his hands clasped as he watched me pull in. He was the cutest boy I had ever seen. This day marked the beginning of our life. I grabbed my letter and barely remembered to turn off the power to the car so the door would open. I popped out of the car and skipped to him like a little kid, waving the paper. He jumped off the table and waited for me to get to our spot.

"Did you get yours? Where is it?" Questions poured out before any greeting, and Mason's eyes twinkled. He had always made fun of me for starting in the middle of a conversation. He grabbed my hand and tugged me into him, covering my mouth with a tender kiss. I threw my arms around his neck and kissed him back, forgetting about the letter. He put his hands on my waist and pulled me closer, deepening the kiss. Bliss momentarily overshadowed my reason for wanting to see him. But only for a moment.

I pulled back. "Mason. Hi. Your letter?"

He kept me in a tight hug and gazed into my eyes. "I've wanted to kiss you since eighth grade."

I swatted his arm. "Then what took so long?"

He leaned in and kissed me again. I lost track of the minutes at that point. It's funny how fuzzy things become when the boy you love kisses you, just as you've always hoped.

Common sense won over, though. I pulled away and put some space between us, letting the cold spring morning air cool the sizzle we had created. I picked up the letter I had dropped and brushed the dirt off, leaving a faint smudge on the bright white paper. "Mason. I got my acceptance letter from Eckman. Did you get yours?"

He gave a soft laugh, then sat down on the picnic table bench. He rubbed his hair and bit his lip. The butterflies that had danced around in my stomach during our kissing session dropped dead and my mouth went dry. Why wasn't he answering? Why did I pop the happy bubble we were in a few minutes ago?

He cleared his throat. "Ah, yeah, I got it. But I also got accepted into the Air Force Academy."

I stared at him, trying to understand the words coming out of his mouth. "The Air Force Academy? Like, the military?"

An amused smile stretched across his face. "Yes, babe. Like the military." He grabbed my hand and tugged me down next to him. "And, um, I'm going to do the air force. Everything is going to be fine. This is a much better opportunity, and it's right near USHA, so only five minutes from here by light rail."

A lump grew in my throat. "But Eckman is on the Western Slope. That's farther than five minutes."

Mason stroked the back of my hand with his thumb. "So it's an hour by bullet train. No big deal. You can come and visit me all the time. Unless you wanted to go to a school down in the Springs. You'd be closer to me then."

Something exploded in me and I jumped up. "Oh, so I have to change all my plans just because you changed yours without even talking to me about it?" I took a giant step back from the table, almost tripping over a pinecone. "I bet your mom forced you to apply, and you did because you refused to tell her you have other ideas about how your life should go."

Mason clenched his jaw. "That's not fair. I've always dreamed of going to the Air Force Academy. My grandpa did, which you would know if you asked."

I huffed out a laugh. "I get it. Your change of plans is my fault. I didn't realize I needed to ask if you were considering doing something other than what you've been discussing for the past year. Cool. Have fun."

I stomped to the car, jumped in, and turned on auto pilot for home, ignoring Mason as he called out behind me. Thank goodness you could program in destinations, because there was no way I could drive myself. Not when my vision was clouded by my dreams going up in smoke.

CHAPTER 8

TRIG STOOD OVER ME, with his eyes closed and his hands stretched above my bed. Not a pleasant way to wake up from a nap. I grabbed a stuffed bear and lobbed it at his head. Bullseye, right in the face.

"Ow, Ash! Geez." He rubbed his nose and glared at me.

"Oh, I'm sorry that I disturbed you after you snuck into my room without asking to be a creeper." I flopped over on my side and faced the wall.

"I was praying for your soul. I mean, you missed church just to sleep in."

"I'm tired. And I did a devo on my own. Go away."

"Did you eat lunch?"

"No."

"Did you eat breakfast?"

"I'm not hungry." My stomach chose that moment to let out a huge growl. I curled up, hoping to mask the sound.

Trig jumped on my bed. "Aha. I was right. Mella, she didn't eat." He yelled that last statement and this time, I growled. In frustration.

I hit him with a throw pillow. "You are the biggest tattle tale. How old are you again?"

"Ash, you have to eat. What's wrong with you? Is this a girl time of the month thing?"

My com chimed three times in a row. I threw a pillow at that too.

"Mason's been trying to reach you all day. He messaged me twice. How does he even have my number?" Trig grabbed my com and swiped at the screen.

I snatched the com. "What can I offer you to go away? I'll do your dish duty from now until the end of school. I'll do your laundry. But only once. That stuff is disgusting."

"Come on, Ash. Spill. What's wrong?"

"I'm not going to Eckman. That's what she's upset about."

I gasped at the sound of Mason's voice. He stood in my doorway, his arms folded.

Trig's eyes widened. "Whoa, man. Are you sure?"

Mason nodded. "I was accepted into the Air Force Academy, and we need to talk about it, but she's ignoring me."

"She won't eat either." Trig reached over and brushed my hair off my shoulder.

I punched the bed. "You two old ladies need to stop talking about me like I'm not here. Trig, I'll eat. Will that make you go away? Mason, just go away."

Trig jumped off the bed. "I'll let you two talk. But I'll be back in ten minutes to drag your sorry body down to the kitchen so I can shove food down your gullet." Then a miracle happened. He actually left.

I clutched my blanket to my chest, very aware of my ratty sweatshirt and the unwashed hair matted around my face. I had nothing to say to him. I mean, I had a thousand words about what a jerk he was for blindsiding me with all these plans to abandon me. But I didn't have the energy for that discussion.

"Ash."

I stared at the bed. "What?"

"Come on. We need to talk."

"So talk."

"Not here. Let's go somewhere. It wouldn't be honorable for me to come into your room."

I snorted. "Ah, the classic military honor."

"Hey. Please. Look at me."

I couldn't resist the longing in his voice. Tears spilled down my cheeks faster than I could wipe them away.

Mason clenched his jaw, his eyes filled with sorrow. "I'm so sorry I sprung all of this on you. I didn't know how to tell you, and it seemed like such a long shot. Please tell me what will make this better."

I huffed out a laugh. "You can go with me to the Storm Chasers rally." The idea flew out of my mouth.

Mason's jaw dropped. "Why would you want to go to that?"

I shrugged. "I want to know what their deal is. And why I've never heard of them before. Wait, do you know about them?"

"Yeah, of course. They're crazy."

I folded my arms. "Well, I still want to go. Julian Hart said there's a rally on Tuesday."

Mason rubbed the back of his neck. "Fine. I'll go with you. Honestly, I don't want to, but I will because I love and support you. Just like I hope you love me and you'll support me."

I sighed, betrayed by the warmth curling in my belly at his declaration of love. "I do love you. And I do want to support you."

Mason's face split into a grin. "Then come on. Let's go get you some food. Nachos, right? Or is it cheesy fries today?"

The dead butterflies in my stomach revived at the sound of Mason knowing what kind of food cheers me up. "Nachos. But, um, I kind of want to wash my hair and change my clothes."

Mason sent a warm look my way that made me want to kiss him. "Change your clothes, but just put your hair in one of those messy things. Washing your hair will take too much time."

I rolled my eyes and looked down at my bed, hoping to hide my smile. "Okay fine."

Loud stomping came from the hallway. "I'm coming up the stairs. I'm getting closer to your room, so whatever you guys are doing, you should stop."

I burst out laughing, and Mason turned around. "I didn't even go in, man. She's coming out for nachos."

Trig appeared next to Mason. "Good. Because she would hate the oatmeal I was about to spoon feed her like an infant."

Mason grabbed Trig and pushed him away. "Five minutes, Ash. Nacho time."

It took longer than five minutes to clean up the hot mess I had going on. I wanted to feel like a human again, and that required mascara, eye liner, and the right shade of lip gloss. But none of that mattered when we were at Cactus Kitchen, the restaurant that doesn't ask questions when you order the biggest plate of nachos on their menu, along with a request to keep their queso coming.

The silence after the server left was awkward. I fiddled with my straw until it became clear that Mason wasn't going to say anything first. "So. The Air Force Academy."

He gave a smile that didn't quite reach his eyes. "Yeah. I really am sorry I never brought it up. There are so many loopholes you have to jump through to get into the Academy. Did you know you have to be in the top three percent of your graduating class? If you're not, you either end up in the Air Force Academy prep school, or with a scholarship to go to a junior college so you can fulfill the academic requirements."

So many things clicked into place. "That explains your intense studying."

He nodded and moved his soda as the server put down the plate of nachos. "I told myself that if I didn't get into the Academy on the first try, then I'd just go to Eckman. But I didn't want to not get in because I didn't do the work."

The nachos no longer looked appealing. "So Eckman has always been a consolation prize."

He reached over and laced his fingers through mine. "Ash. Eckman is a great school. This was just a different opportunity. One that was hard to get. I'm still shocked."

His touch stopped the creeping depression from taking over.

"I think what put me over the top was the letter of recommendation from our US State Representative, since my SAT and ACT scores were the bare minimum that they required. The letters from Mrs. Powers, Mr. San Miguel, and Mr. Udd helped, but that letter from the congresswoman was clutch."

Mason pulled out the center chip of the nachos, taking most of the melted cheese and other toppings with it. I hadn't been successful at training him to work from the outside in when sharing nachos.

"How does the congresswoman even know you?" I pushed the plate closer to Mason. Might as well, since all he had left were naked chips.

"I think Chip wrote the letter, and she signed off on it."

"Chip?" The nachos lost all of their appeal. "What do you mean, Chip?"

Mason took a long drink of soda. Classic Mason, avoiding the question. I could wait him out. I pulled the plate back to me and moved the bowl of queso out of his reach.

"Uh, well, your mom suggested it."

Out of all the shocking things that had happened in my life, that topped the list. "MY mom?"

Mason nodded. "Yeah, I mentioned to her a while ago that I was trying for the Air Force Academy, and she offered to ask Chip to help get a letter of recommendation. Remember, I thought it was a long shot, so I said sure"

"So you talked to my mom about this a long time ago?"

Mason grabbed my hand again. This time, his touch just felt sweaty. "I guess I never told you I had coffee with her. I wanted to tell her my intentions with you, and ask for her blessing."

I wasn't sure my emotions could handle one more dip on this wild rollercoaster. "Intentions?"

"Yeah, Ash. I'm in this for real. Like, I'm not just looking for a good time in high school. I love you, and I wanted your mom to know I'm not playing with your heart."

I grabbed a chip, scooped up some queso, and popped it in my mouth. I needed to think. Mason was saying all the right things and all the wrong things at the exact same time. He loved me and was thinking about our future; that part was what I had always wanted to hear. But he was saying that this next part of our future wasn't together, and I didn't understand how we could build a future apart. On top of all of that, Chip a big part to play in this.

"Also, don't be worried about Chip. He's cool. He even asked me what your mom liked, so I gave him some tips. I think it's what made her finally say yes to going out with him." Mason sat back and grinned as the delicious queso turned sour in my mouth.

He pulled the nachos back to his side of the table and ate as he chattered on about the Air Force Academy, his time line, and all the things he needed to buy. I was numb. My cherished boyfriend shattered my picture perfect view of my future. My mom was dating a slimeball because of my cherished boyfriend. And I only got to eat one naked chip off the plate of nachos because of my cherished boyfriend.

I stopped listening to him and instead turned my thoughts to my dad. He was the only one who could make things right. If he were here, we could expose Chip for who he really is. Which would show Mason that his way into the Air Force Academy was false, and he belonged at Eckman with me.

I needed to find him. Mella was right; he would be here if he could. Which means he was in trouble. The easy road was thinking he had died. But I just knew he was alive.

But where would I even start?

CHAPTER 9

I DIDN'T TELL MY family about the Storm Chasers rally. I didn't want to deal with Mella's patronizing stare, Trig's loud ridicule, or Mom's disapproval. Penn would have been cool with it, but you can't just tell one person something in my family. So I told them I was going out with Mason, and that was it. It seemed deceptive, but technically, it was true. And I was an adult, right? I mean, if I could vote in the upcoming election, then I could go somewhere with my boyfriend without telling anyone where I was going.

I was still overthinking all of this when I smacked face first into Chip's chest on the way to my car. He laughed as he clutched my arms to keep me from falling over onto the driveway.

The temperature in my cheeks grew to an annoying degree. "Oh, um, sorry."

Chip let go of me and grinned. "Ah, to be young and focused again. Off to see Mason? Of course you are. Why else would your focus not be on where you're walking?"

I scowled. "I have a lot of things on my mind."

The amused grin seemed frozen on Chip's face. "Right. Got it. I think this is my Moody Teenager Lesson One. 'Don't draw attention to the follies of youth."

How on earth could Mom stand this guy? I knew the only way to get by him was to play his game. "Congratulations. You get an A. Now, I have to go, so please excuse me."

"Hold on. I actually need to speak with you. Do you have a minute?"

I glanced at the time on my com. "Yeah, a minute, I guess."

Chip took a deep breath and cleared his throat a few times. "I've been able to talk with the other kids one-on-one, but you're pretty busy and hard to nail down." He paused, like he expected me to apologize for that or something. I pressed my lips together. Now was not the time to admit that I made a concentrated effort to be where he wasn't. "I wanted to tell you I'm thrilled to be part of your family. I've watched you all grow up, and you guys are great people. I promise to take care of your mom, and to be the dad that you need."

My jaw fell open, and I gasped. Chip smiled and held out his arms. It took me ten seconds to realize he actually thought I was going to hug him.

"I have a dad."

Chip's smile faltered as he dropped his arms. "I know you did, but since he's not here, I can be there for you. Do all the dad things he wasn't around to do."

I clutched my bag and took a step back. "Look, I get that you mean well, but Dad will be home soon. I guess I'm glad you're willing to take care of us and all, but it won't be necessary."

For an instant, Chip dropped his ridiculous smile and his eyes flashed. Then he huffed out a laugh. "Oh, you poor girl. Livvy said you were the only one still expecting Jonah to come back. Now that you're eighteen, it's time to accept that your dad made some choices that led to him losing his family, and all you can do is move forward."

The heat that had flooded my veins since the moment I smacked into Chip turned to ice. "What do you mean, choices?"

The familiar, arrogant expression resurfaced on Chip's face. Apparently, he could only mask it for a few minutes at a time. "Everything in life happens because of choices, darlin'. The sooner you learn that, the better."

I set my jaw. "What does that have to do with Dad? You mean the choice to see if he could help our country by trying everything he could to stop Goliath?"

He studied me with an intense stare that sent creepy-crawlies down my back. "Yeah, sure. That."

Mom chose that moment to come out of the house. "Hey, guys. What's going on here?"

Chip schooled his features and made doe eyes at her. "Hey, baby. Long time, no see." He pulled her in close and kissed the side of her head.

Mom blushed and playfully pushed him away. "It's still weird that you call me that."

He gave her a tender look. "Well, get used to it, because I'm here to stay."

I gagged. Literally gagged. "Okay, I'm leaving."

Mom reached out and grabbed my coat sleeve. "Hang on. Chip, go on inside. I need a moment to talk to Ashlyn."

He smiled at her and winked at me before slipping inside. I never knew a wink could mean so many things.

I tossed my hair over my shoulder and faced Mom. "What?"

She linked her arm through mine and guided me to my car. "What's up with you? I look out the window and you were looking at Chip like you looked at Trig the time he ate all the crab Rangoon from Hong Hing without sharing any with you."

I glanced at my com. This wasn't the right time to talk about this. I needed to meet Mason so we could get to the rally before it started. "Um, I ran into him on the way to my car. Like, smack into him. He was teasing me."

Mom chuckled. "Oh, honey. Chip is a playful guy. You'll get used to it. No need to shoot eye daggers at him every time he makes a joke."

I yanked my arm away. "And he calls you 'baby?' Isn't he too old to say things like that?"

"Yeah, I'll nip that in the bud." She rolled her eyes. "I've never liked that either, but he's just trying to show me how much he cares."

I forced a smile. "Whatever. I gotta go. I can't be late to meet Mason. He, uh, doesn't have that much time these days with getting ready for the Air Force Academy and all, so I don't want to cut our time short."

"You're handling this so well. Love you, Punkin. See you later. Have fun." Mom drew me into a hug.

I gave her a quick squeeze and got in the car before Chip came back to try to bond with me.

It took me the entire car ride to put the encounter with Chip out of my head. I needed to puzzle that out, but it had to sit on the back burner until after the Storm Chaser rally. I pulled up to Mason's house at the same time he did. I glanced at the clock on the dashboard and jumped out of the car.

"Mason, where have you been? I thought you were waiting for me."

Mason trotted over and gave me a quick side hug. No kisses in front of his mom's house. "I lost track of time. I was with other guys who got into the Air Force Academy. The Academy sent out a list of all the new cadets in our area so we could meet each other. They're cool."

I wrinkled my nose. "Um, great, I guess. Are you ready to go?"

Mason backed toward his house. "I just need to change. I'll be fast, I promise. Come on, you can wait inside."

I folded my arms across my chest. "No, I'll wait out here."

"The breeze is freezing. Come on. I'll be right back."

I sighed and followed him. I wanted to avoid Mason's mom as much as I wanted to avoid Chip. I silently prayed that she wouldn't be home.

"Hello, Ashlyn."

My eyes hadn't even adjusted to the dark interior when I heard my name. Why Mrs. Woods kept her windows darkened at all times, I'll never know.

"Oh, hi Mrs. Woods." I finally saw her sitting in a chair facing the front window. One glance told me that the shading she chose was just enough to let her see the outside world without anyone else seeing her. Which means she was watching us. No wonder Mason only gave me a side hug.

"I heard you got into Eckman University. Congratulations."

I smiled, even though I wasn't sure she could see my face. "Thank you. I've always wanted to go there."

Mrs. Woods clucked her tongue. "I can't believe you babies are college bound. I keep hoping they change the age requirement to twenty-one."

I laughed a little. "Oh no. You mean stay in high school another three years?"

"No, they should make all kids stay at home until they're twenty-one."

I let out a little laugh, then glanced toward the stairs. What was taking Mason so long?

"So, what did you think about Mason's news? Were you surprised?" Mrs. Woods appeared at the edge of the room, finally stepping into the light.

I took a step backward. "Yeah, I was. He didn't tell me he was applying. But after what he's told me, it's really impressive he got in. I mean, of course he did, but it's so great that he met all the requirements."

Her eyes narrowed as she smiled. Her smile reminded me of Chip's. "My dad was an Academy graduate. But we didn't even mention that until the third interview. Mason got in all on his own."

"Oh, nice." I didn't know what else to say.

"Mason is on such a good path now. The Air Force Academy is a four-year program. Then he'll do two two-year deployments overseas to learn about the world. When he finally comes home, he'll meet a nice girl, and they can date for two years before getting married. I think twenty-eight is the perfect age to get married, don't you?"

A rock formed in my stomach. "Oh, um, well, my parents got married the year they graduated college. So I think they were twenty-two?"

Mrs. Woods snorted. "So did I. But with age comes wisdom, hun. For a lasting marriage, maturity is crucial. And everyone needs time to mature. That's just a fact of life."

Seriously, where was Mason? "Yeah, I guess that makes sense."

"I'm so glad that he has a good friend like you. You seem like a loyal person, someone who will encourage her friends to accomplish their goals." Her compliment sounded nice, but had a backhanded feel to it.

"Absolutely."

Mrs. Woods smiled a genuine smile this time. "Oh good. I'm so glad to hear you say that. He will have an easier time in this first phase of his life without distractions, right? Nothing to tie him down, and no one demanding anything that is inappropriate for his age. Nothing could be more inappropriate for him at this point in his life than premature commitment. I want him to fully experience life, and I feel better with your promise to encourage him."

I swallowed hard. Did I promise anything?

She took a step closer to me and dropped her voice. "Listen, I'm not stupid. I know you are extra special to Mason. He's a good-looking kid, so I'm sure you have hopes for him and yourself. But please don't be childish. It's time for you both to grow up and understand how life works. If you truly care about my son, you will set him free to live the life that is best for him. No great story starts out with a high school romance. In fact, it's the high school romances that crash and burn the hardest, the longer you try to hang on to them."

My face flamed. Mrs. Woods had this way of making me feel dirty and ashamed for liking her son. And I had no argument for her.

Mason finally made his appearance. "Hey, it's my two favorite girls." He threw his arm around his mom's neck. Mrs. Woods' face changed as she smiled at him.

"Where are you two off to?"

He let go of his mom and grabbed his com off the table by the front door. "Just a group meeting. It might help with my final project."

Mrs. Woods licked her thumb and rubbed at some spot on Mason's cheek. "Smart. I love how you're finishing school strong, Macy-Mase. Finishing strong means you'll start the Academy strong."

Mason smiled. "Yes, Mom."

"Well, have fun and work hard. Ashlyn, it was nice to talk to you. Oh, you two are driving separately, aren't you? You know you're not allowed to drive teens around."

I nodded once again, feeling like a bobble-head doll. I stepped out and rushed to my car. Mason said goodbye to his mom, then headed to his car before calling out to me. "You know where you're going, right?"

I shook my head. "I came to follow you, remember?" These were our code words for Meet at the park, and we'll ride together from there.

Mason gave me a thumbs up, then turned and waved at his mom who was watching from the porch. He hopped into his car and pulled away. I followed him, vowing to never come to his house again. I didn't need any more blatant reminders that Mrs. Woods hoped I would go out of her son's life forever.

CHAPTER 10

"Ash."

I bristled at the dismay in Mason's voice. "Please don't talk like that. It's condescending."

He pressed his mouth into a firm, straight line as he pulled into the abandoned parking lot at Park Meadows Mall in Lone Tree. "This is super sketchy."

"Then aren't you glad you're with me to keep me safe?" I rubbed his arm. His disapproval would ruin this for me.

Mason parked the car and disengaged the engine. He turned, and his eyes softened when he saw me staring at him. "This spot would be perfect for making out. There isn't anyone around."

I bit my lip. "We'll keep it in mind. But let's go in, okay?"

He frowned. "Go in where?"

I pulled out my com. "The instructions on the site mentioned a brown door without a window on the southwest side of the building. It also said to make sure to park away from other cars."

"Why does it feel like we're the only ones here? I don't like this."

I unclipped my safety harness. "Because a bunch of cars would draw attention."

"More than one car in an empty lot where no one should be?"

"Come on. Please. It starts in ten minutes."

He got out of the car, and a thrill shot through my stomach. I was on the edge of something huge. I was going to get answers. Or at least the right questions to ask to start my search for Dad.

I made myself take normal-sized steps as we headed toward the building as if we were supposed to be there. It felt forbidden to be there. I didn't see anyone watching us. We pulled open the door and stepped into the dark hallway.

It was easy to find the group. One light shone at the end of the row of closed shops, while voices echoed through the empty corridor. We hurried down the hall and stopped at the door.

The room was packed, every chair filled.

"You must be new."

Mason snatched my hand like someone was about to snatch me. I gave his hand a little squeeze and smiled at the short girl snapping her gum in front of us. "Yes, I think. I mean, this is the Storm Chasers rally, right?"

The girl rolled her eyes. "Oh yeah. Totally new. Yes, this is the Storm Chasers rally. Although if you've come to make trouble, you can leave."

My mouth dropped open. "We're not. Why would we make trouble?"

She nodded toward Mason. "Your boyfriend has that look. The one that says he's got a closed mind and will argue with everything we say."

I glanced at him. His face was a thundercloud. I squeezed his hand, hoping he would relax. "I just need some answers."

The girl stared at us for a few heartbeats, then apparently we passed some sort of test. "Alright, come on. I'm Miri Day. You can sit over here."

"I'm Ashlyn, and this is Mason."

"That's cool, I guess."

We followed her to a couple of empty chairs in the last row and had just sat down when the chatter in the room stopped as if someone had flipped a switch.

"That was creepy," Mason said under his breath. I glared at him and turned toward the stage.

Two large men stepped up, each with personal voice enhancers looped around their necks. They both looked the same age as my mom, and also as if they spent ten hours a day in the gym.

"I see some fresh faces," the man with dark hair began. "That's good. We need more on our side if we're going to make any change. I'm Tyler Denzio, and this is Silas Chapman. We've been fighting the fight of the Storm Chasers for almost ten years now, and we think we're about to make a break in the storm."

Cheers and applause broke out. Neither of the men smiled, but nodded at each other like they were expecting this.

The man called Silas stepped forward. "Allow me a moment to recap for those who are new. We have reason to believe that Hurricane Goliath is not natural. By this point, most people have accepted it as a part of our world, but it shouldn't be. Storms are supposed to come and go. Hurricanes get their energy from the warm waters of the Atlantic colliding with the cool air from the north. They would follow the jet stream toward land, where they would lose their power as they hit the shore line. Sure they'd do damage, but the point is they followed a trajectory that ended in their dissipation."

"What caused Hurricane Goliath to behave differently than any other storm?" Tyler stepped up and Silas moved backward. "Meteorologists have debated that very thing through the decades, but no one has ever pointed out that if this were natural, we would have seen a pattern moving toward hurricanes taking longer on land. They never did. Just one day, this big bad wolf showed up and decided he liked it so much, he wanted to stay. It's weird, to say the least."

Murmurs and laughter rose as people discussed this with those sitting closest to them.

Silas raised his hands, and the room instantly calmed back down. "We don't have time to go through the last fifty years to prove why we're right about this. We just need to tell you what we are working on proving today. And we will prove it, because the truth always has a way of coming out."

"We believe that the United States government is using the eye of the hurricane as a secret base. We haven't quite figured out what for yet. Maybe it's a prison for people they just wanted to disappear. Maybe it's a place where the governments of the world meet and make deals that affect our lives but benefit the leaders. We'll figure that out later. But now we are sure we have enough information to prove this."

The lights dimmed and a screen on the wall lit up with a satellite image of the hurricane. I knew that image as well as I knew the family picture on our mantel.

"See this? The date stamp is from two weeks ago."

Another image appeared next to it. "This picture has a date stamp of thirty-five years ago; I was nine years old, for anyone wanting to keep track."

Silas used a laser pointer to highlight spots on each of the images. "Take a look at these spots, here, here, and here. Then look at these cloud formations. Now compare them to the exact spots on the other image. I'll point slowly to each image."

I watched the red dots move from point to point, then gasped along with everyone else. "Mason, they're the same."

He leaned forward in his chair. "I guess"

Tyler clicked the lights back to full power. "They appear the same because they are the same. The picture with the two-week-old date stamp is the same as the one from thirty-five years ago. Whenever they show you pictures of the storm, they aren't showing you current data. They are recycling the images from decades ago."

"So, is the storm still there?" Someone yelled out from the back, causing a dull hum of chatter to break out.

Silas chuckled. "Yes, it's still there. And if you were to go to the Forbidden Zone, you'd see it. But they're reusing data because we'd be able to see the massive structures they've built within the eye."

Tyler's voice echoed above the noise. "We're going to act soon. The United States Hurricane Agency has not been using our tax dollars to find a way to end the storm; they've been using them to keep it going, to fund the military to use as their guard dogs, and to build whatever they want so they can do whatever they want outside the prying eyes of the public."

The chatter grew louder and angrier. "What can we do?" The shouter called out again.

"Join our cause. Spread the word. People accept what the news tells them because they haven't heard anything different. We also need funding, since the government isn't going to give us any. We appreciate any donations you can spare. In three weeks, there will be a vote on Capitol Hill to increase funding for USHA, and it is crucial for us to be there to oppose it. We need sponsors to get our team to Washington."

Mason snorted and leaned back in his chair. "There it is. They just want money."

I glared at him as Tyler wrapped up the meeting. "Thanks for coming, everyone. If you want to stay connected, please sign the tablet by the back door. We'll send out all the new data as soon as we get it, because the more people who have the data, the closer we are to exposing this whole thing. And if we can expose it, then we can shut it down and reclaim that part of the country."

Cheers broke out again as everyone stood to leave. I sat still. Hope blossomed in my chest. "Mason. If there are people in the eye, then my dad must be there."

He cracked up as he stood. "Are you serious?"

His laugh stabbed at my heart. "Yes, I'm serious. I know I can't explain it to you, but I know my dad is alive, and that something is stopping him from getting back to us. Someone must be holding him against his will."

He sat back down and shook his head. "Ash, I love you. But you're grasping at straws here. You just want him to be alive so bad that you'll believe anything anyone tells you."

I was silent for a moment, stunned. Mason had always listened to me. He had never made me feel small and stupid. Until now. I stood up and backed away from him. "Oh, I see. I miss my dad, so I'll probably get into alien abductions next, since that will make the most sense to me, right?"

He jumped up and reached for my hand, lowering his voice. "I didn't mean that. I don't want you to get hurt chasing a dream that won't ever come true."

I yanked my hand away. "You mean like the dream of us going to college together? The dream that wasn't a dream but actual plans until you made your own plans without telling me?"

Mason sighed. "I thought we were past this."

"You wanted us to be past it, so you settled it without even asking." My stomach rolled and a heat wave flashed over me. "How dare you make me accept all the new things that are important to you and dismiss these things that are important to me? I know your mom has coddled you your whole life, but guess what? You are not the center of the universe. Just because your mom taught you that everyone else should bow to your plans doesn't mean it's true."

Mason's jaw set. "I know you're just lashing out because you're upset, but please don't bring my mom into this."

I snorted. "She's been in it the whole time. You know that, right? You've made plans you think are yours, but they're actually hers. And like a good, obedient little boy, you're falling right in line."

Mason stood up straighter. "I make my own decisions, Ashlyn. And also, in case you couldn't tell, this group is anti-military. Did you hear the way they were talking about the bases? If you get involved with them, you're betraying everything I've set my life toward."

I became painfully aware of how loud his voice had become. The room was almost empty, but the few people left were staring at us like we were a free show. "Awesome. You've made this whole thing about you again."

He threw his hands in the air, turned and marched toward the door. "Let's go. We can finish this conversation later."

I plopped down in a chair. "You go. I'm staying. I'll find my own way home."

He stared at me. "Fine. Bye." He disappeared out the door.

After ten seconds, I growled and marched out after him. This was so childish. The door slammed at the end of the hall, and I rolled my eyes and made my way outside.

Mason's car was already gone by the time I got there.

CHAPTER 11

He left me.

My sweet, kind, intentional, non-official-but-everyone-knows-we're-together boyfriend left me in the empty parking lot of an abandoned mall, thirty minutes from home.

A wave of numbness extinguished the anger that had been burning inside. I felt nothing. Except a little thirsty. I laughed when I realized that my water bottle was still in my car at the park. Mella would panic if she knew I left without a water bottle. She acted like a full water bottle was more important than a fully charged com.

I leaned against the wall next to the door and closed my eyes, enjoying the warm sunshine. It was supposed to snow again in a few days, but that was typical for Colorado in March. I'm not sure how many minutes passed by before I remembered I had no way home. Dread curled up in my stomach. Calling anyone in my family was out of the question; they would freak out. I pulled out my com to find Dasha. Maybe she could borrow her mom's car to come get me.

A black screen stared back at me. "What? No! I charged this last night. Didn't I?" I pressed the button on the side a few times, trying to wake it up. These batteries were supposed to last seven days.

"Hey."

I jumped, almost dropping my com. I shoved my hand in my bag, searching for the can of pepper spray that Trig made me keep in there.

A cute boy with dark hair grinned at me. "Sorry. Didn't mean to scare you. I thought me coming out the door and letting it slam shut was enough noise to announce my presence."

A warm flush crept up my neck. I smiled. I couldn't help myself. "I, uh, was pretty focused."

"Obviously. I'm Luca. You're new?"

I nodded. "I'm Ashlyn."

"Cool. Glad you came. What took you so long?" He leaned against the wall and folded his arms like he had all the time in the world.

"Oh, I was trying to see where my friend is to see if she could come pick me up" I stumbled over my words as the flush reached my cheeks. I hoped he'd think the red on my face was from the sun and not from my obvious feelings of foolishness.

His light blue eyes twinkled. I always loved the dark hair and blue eyes combo. Mason's eyes were also blue, but he had blond hair. "No, what took you so long to come to one of our rallies?"

"Oh! Um, I heard about the Storm Chasers for the first time last week."

Luca's grin turned cynical, which took his cuteness down a couple of levels. "Wow. You must have been living under a rock. Did you even know that there was a storm that has been here for 50 years?"

I scowled and tossed my hair. "Of course I did. My mom works for USHA. And my dad disappeared in the storm ten years ago."

His eyes widened, then narrowed. "What did you say your last name was?"

"I didn't."

He studied me for a minute, and I tried to keep my breathing steady. He really was cute, even if he was kind of rude. I mean, his black t-shirt fit his muscular arms perfectly. But I had a boyfriend. Sort of. Not here, though, because he left me. "Let's start over. I'm Luca Denzio. My dad is Tyler Denzio, one of the speakers today."

My jaw dropped, and I leaned toward him. "Whoa, he was your dad? I'm Ashlyn Booker."

"As in, Jonah Booker?"

My mouth was already hanging open in what I'm sure was a very attractive way, and I'm sure I made it prettier by gasping. "You've heard of my dad?"

"We know all the people who have been fighting against the storm, and especially the ones who have gone missing."

"Fighting?" I stepped forward and stopped myself from grabbing his arm. I clutched my bag instead. Real smooth. He probably thought I was afraid he would try to take it from me. "I mean, I guess he was. Mom said he had a theory to stop the storm. What else do you know about him?"

Luca's grin made my palms sweat. "How much time do you have?"

I glanced at my com to check the clock. Still black. "Oh, my com is dead. Which is weird, since it's never died before."

Luca slid his com out of his pocket. "It's almost five o'clock."

I gasped. "Oh no! I need to be home, like, right now. And I don't" I almost told him I didn't have a way home, but that didn't seem wise. Mella would be so proud of my self-awareness. "I mean, I don't have time. Um, can I take a rain check? Or you could message me or something."

Luca's shoulders drooped. Wait, was he disappointed? My heart skipped a beat. "Oh, okay. What's your number?" I rattled it off and watched as he entered it in his com, but he paused before he hit Save. "Hey, weren't you here with some guy?"

I pressed my lips together. "Yeah, that was, um, my friend from school. Mason. He had to leave." That felt like a lie. But I guess Mason and I were just friends. We weren't allowed to be more. I mean, we were friends who kiss. A lot these days. But he did just leave me at an abandoned mall. A real boyfriend wouldn't do that, right?

Luca studied my face and then gave a half smile before hitting Save on his com. "Cool. I'll be in touch. You took the light rail, right?"

I let out a shaky laugh. Of course! The light rail. How could I forget about that? I should have taken that in the first place, rather than having Mason drive me and ruin everything.

"Yeah, I did. I have to go, so I don't miss it."

"Cool." Luca rubbed the back of his neck. "I already said that, didn't I? Uh, I guess I'll see you next time?"

I nodded, unable to come up with anything clever to say. He tucked his com in his back pocket and smiled a heart-melting smile one more time before slipping back inside the brown door.

I stood for a second, then headed toward the entrance of the parking lot. The light rail station was only two blocks away. I hoped this station still had a train that went directly to Castle Rock. If not, I'd have to find a station that did, which would take forever.

The schedule on the screen at the station said a train to Castle Rock would arrive in twenty minutes. I sighed and plopped down on the cold bench. I wished I had stayed to talk to Luca for a bit longer. I could have at least gotten some answers.

Sitting there gave me time to think, though. I was somewhat annoyed that in all of my years of research, I had never considered that the storm wasn't natural. I had wasted so much time studying storms of the early twenty-first century, trying to figure out their pattern to see if I could predict Hurricane Goliath's pattern. Never once did I even imagine I was studying the wrong thing.

How did I not notice that every picture of Goliath was the same? I mean, a storm that is fifty years old is going to look similar, but it should be constantly rotating, which means the cloud shapes will change. No cloud ever held its shape for longer than a few minutes.

"Now that you're eighteen, it's time to accept that your dad made some very poor choices that led to him losing his family, and all you can do is move forward."

I gasped and jumped up, whirling around. Chip's voice boomed, as if he were right behind me. But the station was still empty. I sat down, my heart pounding. What did he mean by that? Luca said that the Storm Chasers consider Dad to be the one who fought against the storm. Is that what Chip meant by making poor choices?

Wasn't the point of USHA to stop the storm? I was proud of my mom's work at that organization. In fact, I believed Dad would be found because of her work there. Even though they had ceased all search and rescue operations years ago, I always believed that Mom would one day find a key to finding Dad.

I glanced at the screen, then back down the street toward the mall. Was Luca still there? I had seven minutes before the train was supposed to arrive. If I ran, I might have time to ask one question. But I wouldn't have time to catch my breath, and there was no way I'd want to heave out my questions like a crazy person. Why didn't I get his number? Oh right, because my com was dead.

The train pulled up before I could figure out how to get there and back again. It was just as well. I needed to get home. I stepped on the empty train, greeted by the most glorious sight: a com charging station. Thanks to Mella's nagging, I always kept a charging cord in my purse, right next to the pepper spray.

I plugged the com in just as the train shot toward home. After a few seconds of charging, the com powered up and four messages came through. I deleted Mason's without even reading it. Two were from Mom, and I fired back a quick "So sorry, on my way" message.

The last message was from an unknown number.

> **Hey, this is Luca. Text me anytime to chat about your dad.**

My eyes filled with tears. Sometimes I just wanted to talk about Dad. My family seemed ready to move on, and besides that, they were too busy to talk about him much anymore. Dasha didn't understand what it was like to have a missing parent. And Mason had never met him.

But Luca knew something about him. And he was willing to talk about him. It took every ounce of self-control I had to play it cool and not message him back right then. I didn't want to seem too eager.

The train pulled up at the station near the park where I left my car, and I bolted out. The first step was getting home. Maybe Mom had some answers, now that I finally knew what questions to ask.

CHAPTER 12

AUTO-PILOT SAVED MY BUTT once again. It took all of my brain power to figure out a delicate way to get information from Mom. The idea that the hurricane is man-made might be upsetting to someone who has dedicated their life to the United States Hurricane Agency for two reasons: one, they might feel foolish if they didn't know, or two, they might feel like a cornered animal if it was information that should have never gotten out. And I needed answers; I didn't want her to shut down.

I was pretty proud of what I had come up with by the time my car self-parked in its usual spot. I forced myself to relax my shoulders and take calm steps in through the front door, only getting distracted for a moment by the delicious pungent aroma of garlic and onion. Darn, I had missed Picante Chicken night. That was one of my favorites.

A deep voice stopped me in my tracks, and I almost groaned out loud. Chip was still here. The thought of Chip eating Picante Chicken now ruined it. I needed to have a talk with her about keeping the Booker family's traditional recipes sacred. I took a slow breath through my nose and rolled my eyes to get it out of my system before pasting the best smile I could on my face.

Mom and Chip were sitting very close at the table. She had her face resting in her hands and her elbows on the table, and she was looking at him with the same bashful, glowing look that cheesy rom-com actresses have on their faces at that point in the movie where they realize they don't hate the lumberjack-dressed hometown boy who they hated in high school. Chip was pinching the tendrils of her hair between his fingers and staring at Mom's lips.

"Uck." I clapped my hand over my mouth as they snapped their heads in my direction. Whoops. I did not mean to let that slip out.

Mom sighed. "Ashlyn."

"Um, sorry. Hi. I just, well, um, hi." My words tripped all over each other as all the logical things I had planned to say vacated my mind. I noticed that neither one of them moved.

"Did your favorite make-out spot lose its magical golden light?" Chip chuckled and glanced at Mom, expecting her to join in the laughter. My chest swelled at the glare she gave him. He dropped his eyes for a moment before peeking back at her. "Sorry."

She scooted away from him. "Ash, you are eighteen, but I would appreciate a little more communication. I don't need to give permission often, but since we still live in community, please tell me ahead of time if I should make dinner for you."

"I'm sorry. My com died, and it took a while to find a charging station."

Mom stiffened and raised her eyebrows. "Where were you that you weren't near a charging station? And why couldn't you just use Mason's com?"

I opened my mouth and shut it twice. I wanted to tell Chip to get lost, but I was trying hard to keep Mom relaxed and open to what I needed to say. "Well, it's kind of a long story. I don't want to bore Chip with the silly teenage details. I'll talk to you later."

He pushed out a chair for me. "No, I want to stay. Being part of this family stuff is what I've been waiting for. Sit, dish."

Before I even had time to react to Chip's cringe-worthy behavior, Trig thundered down the stairs and into the kitchen, bellowing.

"MOM. Ashlyn is missing!" His eyes were wide like he had just seen a ghost, and he looked all sweaty. I couldn't help it; I burst out laughing.

Trig's mouth dropped open when he saw me, and his face twisted into the angriest expression I had ever seen from him. "What are you doing? Mason has been blowing up my phone for an hour. I ignored it because it was just a bunch of random texts like 'Code Lobster,' but then he finally just called and told me he didn't know where you were. Why does he have my number and where were you?"

Just hearing his name crushed any mirth I had over Trig's disheveled appearance. I scowled.

"I thought you were with Mason," Mom said, looking from Trig to me.

The amused look on Chip's face pushed me over the edge. "Well, I was until he ditched me at Park Meadows."

Trig about fell over. "What were you guys doing at an abandoned mall?"

Chip let out a murmur of approval. "That is a good make-out spot."

"We weren't making out," I shouted. "We were at a Storm Chasers meeting, and Mason got mad like a toddler and drove off without me."

That wiped the smile off of Chip's face. Both Mom and Trig became still.

"You were at a Storm Chasers meeting?" Mom said in the quiet voice she used when we were in serious trouble as kids.

"That's your response? Asking if I was at the meeting, and not anything about Mason leaving me somewhere? Yes, I was at the Storm Chasers meeting. And I find it quite interesting that you two work for the United States Hurricane Agency, and yet no one ever thought to mention the Storm Chasers."

Chip snorted. "That's because they're a bunch of idiots. They aren't worth mentioning."

"Who are the idiots? USHA or the Storm Chasers?" I snapped.

Mom clenched her jaw. "Honestly, I don't know where to start."

I pulled out the chair that Chip had pushed toward me and plopped down for a chat. "Fine, let's just forget about Mason. Why don't you two tell me what Dad was working on when he disappeared? I feel like it all boils down to that, anyway."

Mom sat back and pursed her lips. "I think I'd like to talk about this later, when you're calm."

I spread my hands out. "Uh, I AM calm."

Chip put his hand on Mom's arm in a normal, comforting way. "It might be time, Liv. She is eighteen." My heart changed from an angry pounding to a quick, excited skipping beat. Ugh, would this make me start liking him?

Mom jerked her arm away. "Don't forget that it's my job to raise my kids, Chip. There's a line; don't cross it."

I hated how this was turning out. This was the only time in my life that I didn't want Chip to leave, and I was upset that I couldn't rejoice in watching a crack form in the relationship between him and Mom.

He stood up in a calm motion, pressed a kiss to Mom's hair, and said, "I'll call you later, baby." A cloud of heavy, overpriced cologne lingered when he left the kitchen.

Mom squeezed her eyes shut and pinched the bridge of her nose. Never a good sign.

"Mom, I–"

She cut me off by holding up her hand. We sat in silence for a full three minutes before she spoke without opening her eyes. Trig stood like a frozen statue for a bit, as if unsure whether he should stay or go. He backed out of the room, rolling his feet so he wouldn't make any noise. It was a move we had all perfected when Mom was addressing one of us kids and the others wanted to leave before they got in trouble, too.

"I raised you better than this."

It was as if she had slapped me across the face. "What?"

"You don't get to treat guests that way, and you don't get to embarrass me in front of other people."

My memories of Dad were a bit fuzzy since he left when I was so young, but one memory was still clear as a bell. Tears welled up in my eyes as his voice echoed in my ears, repeating the words: "Think before you speak."

But he wasn't here, was he?

I snorted. "What guest? There were no guests here. Just Chip. He's my New Daddy, isn't he?"

Mom heaved a sigh. "Ash, honey. I know you miss your dad. We've been over this. I do too. We always will. The best way to honor him is by finding happiness and moving forward. He did everything he did to make sure that we were happy and cared for, so let's live our lives, okay? Trust me, he would want this."

My hands shook. "But he would never give up on us. Not the way that you all have given up on him."

"This conversation is over." Mom stood up.

"No! Tell me what Dad was working on!"

Mom walked out of the kitchen without a backward glance.

I buried my head in my hands and sat in the silent kitchen, listening to the hum of the fridge. It made a weird cyclic hum, starting low and sliding up.

I don't know how long I sat there until someone came in. I kept my eyes on the table and my ears tuned to the song of the fridge. They sat next to me in a chair for a while, then moved around the kitchen. They opened the door to the fridge, which cut off the song mid-verse. They also opened and shut the food cooker. The song it sang was much louder than the song of the fridge. The smell of Picante Chicken once again filled the kitchen, mingling with Chip's leftover cologne bomb.

My stomach growled just as a plate slid under my bent head. I peeked up as Trig sat down across from me.

"Eat."

I stared at the plate. "I don't have a fork. Or a knife. Or a drink."

He let out an exaggerated sigh, got up, and stomped around the kitchen while I stared at the cheese melting into the salsa rice. He smacked a fork and knife on the table, then slid a glass of water toward me.

"Thanks." The first bite of chicken tasted like my childhood.

"Ash. Did Mason really leave you at a Storm Chasers meeting? Because this is, like, Strike Three material."

I chewed and swallowed. "Yes, he did. He thought they were disrespecting the military. Because he is now military."

"Were they?"

I rolled my eyes. "No. They said that they thought the government was hiding something in the eye of the hurricane, and the military was their guard dog."

Trig stared at me.

I shoved another bite of the delicious cheesy chicken and rice in my mouth and talked around it. "They said that the hurricane is man-made, and that there is probably some kind of compound in the eye. We can't see it, because the pics and videos they show us are recycled. We're not seeing new pictures anymore, so we're not getting accurate information about what is in the center."

I finished the rest of my dinner in silence while Trig sat with me. He really was my favorite. Mella would have ignored the part about the Storm Chasers and Mason and started lecturing me on the importance of having my com charged. Penn would have ignored everything and eaten half of my dinner. And we all know how Mom handled it.

I rinsed my plate and put it in the dishwasher, then turned to Trig. "Go ahead. Say whatever it is you've been working on for the past five minutes."

He scratched his chin. "I guess all I want to say is, change is hard. You're dealing with it in the best way you know how. But be careful. Don't let Mason get away with crap. And don't just latch on to things because they are what you want to hear."

My com chimed before I could respond, and I looked at the display.

"Go talk to him, so he stops bugging me. And remember, no matter where I am, I'm always here for you."

I rolled my eyes. "Okay, Uncle Trig. Thanks."

I hurried up to my room and closed myself in, leaning against the door as I pulled up the newest text. It wasn't from Mason.

> **One more thing...there's another Storm Chasers meeting on Friday, if you want to come.**

A soft tap rapped on my door. I whirled around, almost dropping my com.

"Yeah?"

Mom poked her head in. "Can I come in?"

I pushed aside my bruised, tender feelings and nodded. She crossed the room and sat on my bed.

"Ashlyn, I'm sorry for walking out on our conversation. That was unkind, and not very mature."

I nodded. "I forgive you. And I'm sorry for being rude to Chip. I wasn't thinking before I spoke."

Mom gave a small smile. "I forgive you." She patted the bed, and I went and sat next to her. "Sweetheart, I've told you all I can about your dad. I realize that's not what you want to hear, but it's the truth."

"But maybe Chip knows more," I whispered.

"Maybe. And I wouldn't object to you asking him about it. But not when you're so antagonistic toward him. You catch more flies with honey."

I let out a mirthless laugh. "Yeah."

She wrapped her arm around my shoulders. "Do you want to talk about Mason?"

I shook my head. "I'll talk to him tomorrow or something."

She kissed my hair. "If you change your mind, let me know." She stood to leave, then turned back. "And Ash, I don't mind you going to the Storm Chasers' rallies. They might help you, although I don't think they'll give you the answers you're hoping for. But you need to go for yourself. Just be safe, okay?"

Mom was full of surprises. I never dreamed she'd give me her blessing. I jumped up and gave her a hug. "I will. I promise."

She squeezed me back. "Love you, Mini-Muffin."

"Love you, too."

She shut the door behind her as she left, and my heart felt light. I pulled up the text from Luca and sent my reply.

I'll be there.

CHAPTER 13

MELLA WAS A GREAT CNA, and would make an excellent nurse, but I think she missed her calling. She would have made an excellent member of the SWAT team. They would have approved of the amount of force she used on my unlocked bedroom door while I was getting ready for school the next morning.

"Storm Chasers?"

I didn't pause digging through my earrings to find that pair that Dasha had given me for Christmas.

"What's the question? That they exist? Because they do, even though no one ever told me about them. Pretending something doesn't exist doesn't mean it doesn't exist."

She perched on the edge of my bed. "But you actually went to one of their meetings?"

I sighed and turned to face her. "Yes, I did. And I'm going to another one on Friday. Do you want to come with me?"

She pressed her lips together. "Are you trying to hurt Mom because she's with Chip?"

"What? No!"

"You are aware that attending their meetings betrays the family, right?"

I raised an eyebrow. "Are you joking? How is going to a meeting betraying the family?"

"Think about it. Mom and Dad devoted their life to USHA. The Storm Chasers are doing everything in their power to undermine what USHA does. Why would you take part in that?"

At that moment, I was tired of defending myself. My throat squeezed tight, and I took a deep breath in through my nose to stave off the tears pressing against my eyes. Why couldn't anyone understand? Or at least try?

"I'm not blaming Mom for anything or trying to ruin her career. What if there's game-changing information out there? That could help us find Dad? Something that even Mom doesn't know because she's too busy doing her own job and taking care of us? Shouldn't we learn and hear every perspective?"

Mella sighed and handed me a tissue. "Sometimes it's good to get information, and sometimes the information can just be unnecessarily confusing. I'm telling you, everything you're searching for is going to lead back to the same conclusion—"

I held up my hand. "Do not say it. I don't need to hear it again. Forget I asked. Never mind. Tell me about your new apartment or whatever instead, okay?" I had no one to blame but myself. Asking her to go with me was a terrible idea.

Mella stared at me through squinted eyes for a few seconds. "Do you truly want to hear? Because I feel like you're just changing the subject."

"Of course I do. And yes, I am changing the subject. I have taken to heart all you have said about how our lives are moving on. Tell me about your new place so I can get excited, alright?"

I don't know where that flash of brilliance came from, but it worked. Mella flopped on my bed and rattled on about her condo and where she planned to get furniture to fill it. I nodded, smiled, and laughed at the right times, avoiding commitment to help clean before she moves in.

I should have expected Mella's reaction. I did not expect how my friends would react to my invitation.

"Gretchen, stop laughing." I sighed as I watched her roll around on the ground. "That floor is disgusting. You should get up."

She let out one final snort. "I'm sorry, but I couldn't help it. What a hilarious idea. Let's go to the rally, and then afterward we can hit up the Flat Earthers BBQ."

Rosalie clutched my arm. "Wait, are you serious? She's serious, Gretch. Shut up."

Gretchen sat up, a blush staining her cheeks. "Oh my gosh. Ash. I thought you were joking."

I reached out my hand and pulled her off the floor. "I get it. But I am serious. I went yesterday. They have new information I'm curious about. It could help me find my dad, you know?"

Rosalie and Gretchen exchanged glances. Rosalie cleared her throat. "We were gonna go to the basketball game on Friday. It's the playoffs, and it might be the last game that we'll ever see in high school."

"Yeah, who knows if Rosie will ever see Zed all sweaty in his uniform again?" Gretchen tried to keep a straight face, but burst out laughing when Rosalie pushed her over.

I pasted on a smile. "Oh, I totally get it. Of course, you should go to the basketball game. It's not a big deal. No worries."

Rosalie placed her hands on either side of my head, gazing into my eyes. "Are you sure?"

I grabbed her head in the same way. "Yes. Especially if they win, and Zed finally grabs you and kisses you in his joy, and it ends this ridiculous tension of Will They Won't They. I'm dying for that to be over so we can all enjoy the last few weeks of senior year."

Rosalie tossed my hands away and blushed. "We'll see, won't we?"

Dasha rushed up, typing on her com. "I have two seconds. Catch me up."

"Ash wants someone to go with her to the Storm Chasers Rally on Friday, but Rosie and I are going to the basketball game so that maybe Zed will kiss her," Gretchen summed up.

Dasha glanced up from her com. "Oookay."

I bit my lip. "Can you come with me?"

"I can't. I mean, of course I would, but I have a big test in History of Interior Design that will go until like, five o'clock, and then Mom made me promise on my com that I'd be at dinner that night because 'the Harts don't go over four days without dinner together.'" She rolled her eyes. "It's been a busy week, and you know how Mom gets."

I channeled the pasted smile again. "Of course I do. I'm Team Momma Hart, so do what you have to do to make her happy."

Dasha threw her arm around my shoulders. "Is Mason going with you?"

My chest tightened. I hadn't seen him yet today, but I didn't feel like getting into that with my friends. "Uh, yeah, probably. I was kind of hoping to make it a girls' night, but I guess a date night could be fun, too."

Dasha narrowed her eyes. "What aren't you telling me?" Gretchen and Rosalie tightened the circle, all joking gone.

"I haven't seen him today. Usually, he's a barnacle attached to your hip," Gretchen said.

I shrugged and laughed a little. "Everything is fine. He had work to catch up on. Did you know you have to be in the top three percent of your class to be accepted into the Air Force Academy? He just wants to make sure he doesn't fall out of that in these last weeks of school."

Rosalie's mouth dropped open. "Whoa. I always thought he was a stickler about studying because of his mom."

I let the conversation evolve into an assessment about Mason's mother. Normally I would have tried to change the topic out of respect for who I had always hoped would be my future mother-in-law, but I wasn't feeling so charitable about that family today. I did my best to laugh at their jokes and observations, but my stomach hurt. None of the important people in my life were willing to go to something important to me.

So I went by myself. I drove to Park Meadows and turned off the Family Finder feature on both the car and my com. I didn't want Mason tracking me. I took a moment to wonder what the mall looked like on a normal Friday afternoon during its heyday. Now the train shot right past this area, leaving it as empty as it had looked on Tuesday.

I walked into the building and headed straight to the room. Despite the empty parking lot, people spilled into the hallway, which was surprising. I squeezed around them and peeked inside.

Every chair already had a body in it and people lined the back wall. I mentally kicked myself for not trying to show up earlier.

"Hey! Booker!" The mid-level hum of chatter died down as individuals stopped talking amongst themselves and all the faces turned toward the door. My cheeks burned as I scanned the room, looking for who could have called out my name.

Luca stood and waved from a table by the stage. I swallowed, smiled at nearby people, and tried to make my way through the crowd. The murmuring increased as I approached the table.

"Hey," I said. I looked over my shoulder. "Thanks for that. Now everyone is staring. Do you call out all the latecomers?"

He sat down and pushed out the chair next to him. The only empty chair in the entire room. "They're staring because of your name. Everyone knows the name Booker. I could have called out 'Myrtle', but then you wouldn't have answered."

A feeling of unreality washed over me. How had I lived my whole life without knowing that my dad was famous? I guess I had never thought about it, being a little kid and all. But then again, thousands had gone missing in the storm, especially right at the beginning. I never heard my dad's name mentioned in reports or broadcasts. If they talked about him once, they had moved on. The same way my family seemed to.

I didn't know how to process being famous in a room. "So, why isn't anyone sitting next to you?"

His mouth tipped up in an adorable half-grin. "Miri was, but she left to go drum up business." He tipped his head toward the back of the room, where Miri was talking with wild gestures to a couple of shell-shocked people. "Her enthusiasm knows no bounds."

"What business is she drumming up?"

He slid a clipboard across the table. "We need sponsors for the trip to D.C. to protest at the vote for the USHA funds. And volunteers. They need to come sign up, but no one was making a move."

"Are you related to Jonah Booker?"

Luca and I both jumped. Five people had suddenly appeared at the table. I looked at Luca, and he laughed. "He doesn't mean me."

I swallowed. "Yes. He was, I mean, is, my dad."

Miri darted around the group. "See, I told you! This is Ashlyn Booker, everyone. Her dad was the first Storm Chaser who went into the storm to prove that the government has been lying about it all along."

My breath caught in a hitch. Was that even true, or were they just using me and my dad to get people over to the table? Luca put his hand on my arm and leaned in close. "Hey, we can talk about this later. I promise. For now, just smile and nod, okay? Please?"

An uncomfortable silence lingered as I glanced at Luca. He held my eyes and waited. He smelled so good. I snapped my mouth shut and pressed it into a smile, then nodded at the group that had tripled in size.

Luca handed me a clipboard and held another one up. "We need sponsors and volunteers for the march on Washington, D.C. They are voting to increase funding for

USHA, and that money needs to stop! Please sign up to help however you can."

A lady squeezed past the crowd and leaned toward me. "How old were you when he went missing, hon?"

My vision blurred. "Eight. He disappeared just after my eighth birthday."

She tsked and gave me the look of pity that I hadn't seen since then. "Goodness, you've had to come of age without him, haven't you?"

Tears pressed at the back of my eyes and I nodded again. "The Storm Chasers think people are in the eye. My dad might be there. If we want to get to them, then we must first find a way around USHA."

The woman grabbed my clipboard. "Well, I'll help however I can. The hurricane is absurd. We shouldn't tolerate it just because the government said so."

The noise of the crowd rose as they all chimed in their agreement. For the next thirty minutes, people bombarded our table with sign-ups to support the march and anything else Luca could think of.

The crowd finally thinned out, and I handed the clipboard to the last person in line, who snatched it as if I had been the one stealing it.

"Who do you think you are?" Tyler Denzio frowned at me, and I shrunk back.

Luca stood up. "Dad, this is Ashlyn Booker. Jonah Booker's daughter. She's been helping."

Tyler grabbed Luca's clipboard, too. "Son, you know better than anyone that we have to vet all volunteers. Especially volunteers who say they're someone important."

The nerve of this guy pushed me over the edge. "Excuse me. First, I never said I was important. And it seems to me that before I sat here, you had zero help. Now those clipboards are full. Are you sure you're willing to give up that over something as dumb as protocol?"

The sweet lady I first talked to marched up to the table. "Typical government behavior, right there. I'm not here to work with the government."

Tyler narrowed his eyes. "We've been burned by imposters before. This cause is more important than that."

I stood up and folded my arms. "You're right. And I'm not here to hurt any cause. I just want to find my dad. My name is Ashlyn Booker, and my dad is Jonah Booker. I am happy to go through whatever process you have."

The lady started clapping, and soon everyone was cheering. My cheeks grew warm, and I sat back down. Silas hopped up on stage, his voice amplifier activated. "Okay, everyone, let's not waste anyone's time. Let's get started."

Tyler's face softened, and he jumped up on stage with Silas to begin the meeting.

Luca squeezed my shoulder. "That was awesome."

I gave him a look. "I need to know what you all know, and what you're telling everyone. Like, now."

He nodded. "Let's just get to the end of this meeting, then we can go somewhere. Okay?"

I only had a flash of a feeling that said I shouldn't go anywhere with someone who was still a stranger. But it was too late for caution. It was time for answers. "Okay."

Chapter 14

LUCA LAUGHED AS MY com buzzed for the seventh time. I rolled my eyes, picked it up and sent the first emoji that popped up.

"Sorry."

"No, don't be." He grinned. "I'm glad your friend is so worried about you. If Miri said she was hanging out with a guy she had just met, I would feel the same."

Apparently, I couldn't ignore Mella's nagging voice inside my head about "staying safe" and "stranger danger," so I messaged Dasha that Luca and I were hanging out for a bit at the abandoned food court at Park Meadows. I thought she'd just give me a thumbs up and go back to the Hart Family Game night, but she freaked out and said she would message me every five minutes, and if I didn't respond she would call the cops or worse, call Mella.

Would she have felt better knowing it wasn't abandoned? There were Storm Chasers all over the cavernous room, in groups surrounding the giant fireplace in the middle. A fireplace seemed like a cozy, weird place to eat fast food. And Luca's dad was sitting ten tables over, staring at us. I guess that was part of the vetting process.

I put down the com and leaned toward Luca. "I have about five minutes left before Dasha files a missing person report. So let me get this straight…Silas's brother Mateo worked with my dad at USHA."

He nodded. "Jonah was the first one ever to suggest that Goliath isn't natural. Mateo and Jonah knew they would need solid proof if anyone was going to take them seriously. So they planned a research trip inside the storm, even though by that time USHA was putting the breaks on spending on those kinds of trips. Somehow it got a green light, and well, you know what happened. Your dad never made it out. Mateo was convinced that the only reason USHA approved of the trip was so they could eliminate him and your dad. Mateo didn't go due to a sinus infection. As soon as they called off the search, Mateo quit USHA and formed the Storm Chasers."

I rubbed my eyes. "I can't understand why Mom hasn't mentioned this. The only thing she ever said was he had a theory on how to stop the storm, but never anything about the storm not being natural."

Luca shrugged. "From what I understand, Mateo and Jonah kept it super quiet, because what they were suggesting was dangerous. I don't think they even told their wives."

That didn't sit right with me. It didn't seem like my parents kept secrets from each other. From us kids, yes. Not each other. But it would have meant that my mom kept it a secret from us all these years. Was that the better option?

Then again, Mom said she had told me everything about Dad that she could. Did she have more knowledge than she let on? The real question is, did they say anything to

Chip? Chip was supposed to be Dad's best friend. Too many questions were stacking up.

Before I could ask any of them, my com buzzed again, a full two minutes early. I snatched it up and pressed the call back button.

"Dash, I'm fine. I promise. I'll leave in five minutes and head straight to your house, okay?"

"Ash?"

I froze at the sound of Mason's voice.

"Uh, hi. I thought you were Dasha."

"I figured. If you're not with Dasha, where are you? I'm at your house and no one is here. Why did you turn off your com tracker?"

I turned my back to Luca, as if that action alone made my conversation private.

"I can't talk right now. I'll call you later, okay?"

"Will you? Are you done giving me the silent treatment?"

"You. Left. Me."

"I know. I'm sorry, Ash. This is what I wanted to say: I'm so sorry. For leaving you. Will you forgive me?"

He did sound sincere. The ice around my heart started to thaw.

"Um, maybe. I have to go. Maybe call me tomorrow?" It was the best I could do.

"Yeah, okay. Bye. Love you."

I swallowed and ended the call without saying "love you" back.

"Was that the guy you were with when you came to your first meeting?"

I whipped around. "You remember him?"

Luca gave a half-grin. "Of course. He looked like he wanted to burn the place down with us inside. We're trained to watch for people like that."

A rush of heat surged through my body. "Well, your dad wasn't saying very nice things about the military. He practically called them mindless puppets. And Mason just got accepted to the Air Force Academy. Only, like, ten percent of applicants make it."

He held his hand up. "Okay, okay. I'm sorry. I get it."

"Luca. Let's go. We have two minutes to check in." Tyler stood with his arms across his chest.

Luca sighed. "Sorry. Gotta go. Dad and I have to walk through the mall and check in with the owners. They hired us to provide security for this place, and that's why the Storm Chasers use it for our meetings."

I calmed down. "Oh. I wondered how you could use this mall."

"Well, they don't exactly know we do. So keep that to yourself, okay?"

I nodded and stood. "Thanks for the info."

Luca stepped closer. "I'm sorry for insulting your friend. I didn't mean to. We tend to operate from a place of defensiveness, but I'm starting to see how off-putting that is."

His maturity melted my defenses. "No, I get it. Anyway, I guess I'll see you around."

"Yeah, okay. Um, get home safe." For the first time, he seemed to stumble over his words.

Tyler cleared his throat, and Luca hustled away.

I drifted through the next week as I watched my siblings pack up their meager belongings. When they said they were moving, they meant it. All of them planned to be out by the end of the month. Mella was already moving things into her new apartment.

I helped Mella carry a few boxes to her car on Thursday afternoon. The mood had been fun and light. Despite my own sadness, her excitement was contagious. It was clear that this was the right move. It was time for her to build her own life.

It took too long to realize this would be good for me. With Mella out of my space, I could do real research on the Storm Chasers and on Dad's days at USHA without her looking over my shoulder.

"I can't believe how good you're being about all this," she said as she shoved a box into her crammed trunk.

I rolled my eyes. "I'm an adult now, Mel."

She closed the trunk and smacked the top in victory. "Yeah, but you were so upset, and then you made this one eighty. What changed?"

I shrugged. "What can I say? When you're right, you're right."

She threw her arm around my shoulders and guided me back to the house. "And how are you doing with Mom and Chip?"

All my settled resolve about her moving out sank like rocks in my stomach. I thought about telling her what I heard Chip say in the office that day, but she would dismiss it. "Look, I am not going to dance for joy about that now. Okay? Just give me some space, please."

She studied my face, as if she were looking for something to pounce on. Then she sighed. "Okay. I guess it's been good that he's been out of town. I'll admit that it felt weird for him to suddenly be here all. The. Time."

"Right? That's what I'm saying."

Just then, Dasha zoomed her car to a stop in front of the house. Saved by Dasha.

I waved at her and held up a finger. "I gotta go, Mel. Dash and I are going to the library to do some work on our senior projects."

Mella frowned at Dasha. "Tell her to obey basic traffic laws, okay?"

I rolled my eyes, then ran inside for my bag with my tablet and com before heading out and jumping in the front seat of Dasha's car.

Dasha pulled away, her eyes on her rearview mirror. "Why does Mella always watch me drive away like that?"

I changed the music to a new playlist. "Because she thinks you're going to crash and we'll all die."

She glanced at me. "These cars practically drive themselves. I'm not sure I could crash it if I wanted to."

I laughed as she plugged in the address to the library and hit Auto Pilot.

The library in Castle Rock was one of the last remaining libraries in the state of Colorado. I loved working there because it was so quiet. It was like being in a museum. There was no where else you could find so many books. I mean, I had thousands of books on my tablet, but there was something about sitting in the middle of the towering shelves filled with real paper books.

The funny part was, we were still doing most of our research on the internet. We hoped to find an old source in the library. Our teachers always acted like we were brilliant when we cited a reference from a hard copy of a book.

I plunked my bag down on a table and pulled out my tablet. "How much work do you have left on your project?"

"Oh, I'm almost done, but first, I need to look up a few more shops for us to visit in Seattle." Dasha grinned.

I laughed. "What shops?"

She typed something on her tablet. "Thrift shops. I've heard that there are some great vintage thrift shops near where we're staying. If anything, I want some inspo for pulling the Pacific Northwest vibe into my interior decorating. I think it will give me an edge here, don't you?"

I nodded. "Oh yeah. The mountain vibe we've got here is so overdone."

She narrowed her eyes. "I can tell you're making fun of me, but I'll let it slide."

I was glad when she went back to her research. I wanted to do research on my own, but not on my senior project.

I logged onto the library's database and typed in "Hurricane Goliath." The resources listed on the first page were all ones I had seen before. They all said the same thing, anyway.

Then I smacked my forehead. Why had I never thought to search for my dad? I typed in "Hurricane Goliath and Jonah Booker" and within seconds, I had several dozen articles I had never seen before.

"What are you doing?"

I jumped at Dasha's voice, so close to my ear. I tipped my tablet so she would stop reading over my shoulder. "Research."

She pushed her eyebrows together and tightened her lips. "Ash."

"Do NOT say it. Do not say it's time to move on. Because it's not. I need to follow up on new information."

"What do you mean?"

"I met some people at the Storm Chaser rally. They told me that the reason USHA approved Dad's trip was so they could get rid of him."

Her eyes widened. "But how do they know?"

"Because one of the leader's dad was a person who worked with my dad. He quit at USHA right after Dad went missing and started the Storm Chasers."

"Who told you this?"

I hesitated. I hadn't told Dasha about Luca, and I wasn't sure I wanted to. What if she didn't understand? Telling her about Luca meant revealing how I met him, which also meant sharing Mason's abandonment. She would not take that well. Then I'd have to tell her about Mason and me not speaking all week. And even though I was still mad at Mason, I didn't want anyone else to be. I wanted to protect him.

"Silas Chapman is one of the leaders of the Storm Chasers, and his brother was Mateo. Mateo worked with my dad, and I wanted to verify that."

She studied my face. "What aren't you telling me?"

"Nothing! Look." I quickly typed "Jonah Booker Mateo Chapman USHA" into the tablet as Dasha scooted over to my side of the table. We gasped at the same time.

The very first article that popped up had the headline "Deputy Director of USHA Goes Missing in Hurricane Goliath."

> **United States Hurricane Agency Deputy Director Jonah Booker is reported missing in Hurricane Goliath. His exploratory expedition lost contact with base control ten hours after he entered the storm.**
>
> **Mateo Chapman, the assistant deputy director, was set to be part of the expedition team but had to drop out due to a sinus infection on the eve of the storm.**
>
> **"We knew the mission was dangerous, but we expected to be in contact for at least twenty-four more hours," Chapman said. "All the data pointed toward a weakened path that would have allowed safe travel for at least fifty miles."**
>
> **Rescue efforts are underway. Director Chip Sinclair has not commented on the rescue mission's prognosis.**

"Your dad was the deputy director?" Dasha squeaked.

I clicked out to the search results, and the first four headlines gave him the same title. "How did I not know this?"

Dasha typed the same search into her tablet. "Children usually have no idea about their parents' jobs, right? I mean, I thought my mom was just a teacher for a long time. I didn't know that she was the principal. You don't ask what you don't know to ask, right?"

My com buzzed, and I picked it up.

Go out with me tomorrow night? Dinner?

The text from Mason threw me off. He had never been so straightforward in asking me out. Usually, we made it sound like a group thing, so his mom wouldn't forbid him from going. My heart fluttered, despite how upset I still was with him. Making it formal was his way of truly expressing his apology.

Okay

"What's with that smile?" Dasha leaned over and looked at my com. "Oh." She grinned and made kissy sounds.

I shoved her shoulder and turned back to my tablet. Finally, things were going in the right direction. Mason and I were going to make up, and I was on track to getting new information about Dad. New information could lead to the right information.

Chapter 15

I HAD BEEN WATCHING out the window for ten minutes. It was a risk; Trig would make fun of me if he saw what I was doing. Let's see...this time would be something about a princess waiting for her knight in shining armor. He had been on a real medieval kick lately. Sometimes I didn't want to be teased.

I flew down the stairs as soon as Mason's car entered the cul-de-sac, calling out that I was leaving. Trig and Mom were the only ones home, but I didn't want them to intercept him. Things were still so raw and tender.

I was at the end of the driveway just as he pulled up. I surprised him by opening the door before he could shut off the car.

"Whoa. Hey," he said.

I took a deep breath and shifted to face him. "Hey."

The silence made my mouth turn dry. I tried to relax my shoulders. That's the thing about your first boyfriend. You have no practice on how to resolve things after a fight.

He reached over and grabbed my hand. I hadn't realized how tightly I had been clenching my fist until he put his hand on mine.

"Ashlyn. I am so sorry."

I lifted my eyes to his, my heart melting at the pleading look. I laced my fingers through his. "I forgive you."

"Do you?" He released my hand and gently brushed my hair off of my face.

I nodded and leaned toward him, tipping my chin up. He took the hint and cupped his hand around my cheek before pressing his lips to mine in the softest, sweetest kiss he had ever given me.

So this was how to make up with your boyfriend. Apologies and kisses. Both were magic.

Mason broke the kiss and pressed his forehead to mine. "Okay, then."

"Okay," I echoed. "So, where are we going?"

"I don't know. Where do you want to go?"

I leaned back in my seat. I didn't want to be bossy or demanding. I also wasn't sure if he was paying, since we hadn't ever been on a formal date before. If he was paying, I needed to make sure I wasn't picking something that was too expensive. Trig always made fun of me for having expensive tastes. I enjoyed ordering steak while out with my family, and I wanted a soda, even with free water available. I had learned long ago to stop asking to order appetizers.

And if we were paying for our own, I needed to be careful. I didn't have many funds left in my account, and I wanted to save as much as I could for the senior trip. "Um, where do you want to go?"

Mason shrugged. "What do you feel like?"

I wished he would just say a place. Offer any kind of idea of what he was thinking. "Anything, I guess."

"Then how about Cafe Disco? I have a two-for-one coupon."

My stomach dropped. Sandwiches. He picked sandwiches for dinner as our first date. I had never liked anything from there. "Yeah. That would be fine."

Mason's cute little dimple appeared as he powered up the car. Okay, fine. I'd eat a free sandwich with him if it made him smile like that.

We made small talk on the way to the restaurant, but I noticed we avoided talking about what we had been doing for the past week. We may have kissed and made up, but that didn't solve our problem.

At Cafe Disco, I got what I wanted, a steak and cheese. It was the most expensive sandwich on the menu, but I figured since he had a coupon, it still made for a cheap date. Sure enough, he ordered the least expensive sandwich. This could be good; we could balance each other out.

I grabbed some napkins and claimed the booth in the back corner while he waited at the counter for our food. I couldn't help but notice the girls working behind the counter were staring at Mason. His manners, intentional eye contact, and calm smile were hard to resist. One girl leaned in and giggled when handing him our food. Classic flirt move. Based on the dirty look she shot at me, he must not have responded the way she was hoping. Pride swelled in my chest. He was with me.

After we had settled with our food, Mason took a deep breath. "Can we talk things out?"

The bite of sandwich I had taken turned dry in my mouth, and I reached for my soda. "Okay."

He picked at his bread. "I am sorry for leaving you. It was wrong, and I shouldn't have done it. The Storm Chasers disrespected everything I stand for, and I was disappointed you sided with them instead of me."

I swallowed and tried to think before speaking. "I didn't mean to make you feel that way. I don't agree that they were disrespectful, but I understand why you might think so."

He shoved a bite in his mouth. "But they were being disrespectful. They said that the government has been lying to the American people. The same government that I'm about to swear to defend."

The sandwich in front of me lost all of its appeal. "You can defend them without agreeing with everything they do, can't you? Or are you saying that our military are mindless drones who have to celebrate every poor, misguided, or self-serving idea that the government comes up with?"

He paused and took a big breath. "This is not going how I thought."

"How did you think it would go? That you would say you're sorry, and kiss me like that, and buy me a sandwich with a coupon, and I would bow down and let you decide for me how I should think?"

He pulled a small piece of paper out of his pocket. "Um, sorry, I had a few points I wanted to remember."

I laughed in astonishment. "You brought notes?"

Mason looked at me with pleading eyes. "Ashlyn, I love you. And I'm trying to make sure that we're working through things like adults. And I was afraid that I would forget what I wanted to say. Don't you want to hear what I have to say?"

That sobered me. He was trying so hard, even if he was making so many mistakes. I got up from my side of the booth and slid next to him. "Yes, I do. I love you too. I'm sorry. Okay, I've heard your point of view; will you listen to mine?"

He nodded.

"Here's the thing. I truly believe my dad is still alive. And for the first time, I'm learning things that are giving me hope I can prove it. Yes, the Storm Chasers may have messed up ideas about the military or USHA, but that doesn't make everything they say wrong, does it?"

He shrugged. "I guess not. But I don't understand how you can trust them."

"I have no reason not to, for now. And I'm not saying that everything they say is 100% the truth, but isn't it worth looking into for longer than a day?"

He crushed a napkin in his hand just as my com buzzed. I pulled it out and saw that Luca had sent a message. My heart gave a skip, and I froze. I couldn't read a message from Luca while I was on a date with Mason. But what did he want?

Mason huffed. "What are you doing? Didn't you know that looking at your com while on a date is rude?"

I glared, then returned to the booth's other side. "So I'm not supposed to check if my mom needs me? What if something is happening at home?"

He let out a snort. "Mom was right; girls can't live without their coms anymore. Would you give me your focus if I texted you right now instead of trying to talk face to face?"

All my hopes that I had been making headway with Mrs. Woods crashed to the ground. Is this how she talked about me? Just lumping me in with the faceless masses? Would she ever accept me as a part of her son's life?

I folded the wrapping around my sandwich. "I'm done. Can you take me home now?"

Mason reached across and grabbed my hand. "Ash, I'm sorry. I don't know why I said that."

I gave him a sad smile. "I'm going to be honest. I don't know how to work things out with you. I want to, but I just don't know how."

"I think we just have to keep talking."

"But what do we do when we don't agree?"

"I don't know either, I guess." He let go of my hand.

I picked up my sandwich. "I'm really tired. Can we go?"

He nodded and collected his trash. The car ride home was quiet, but not as awkward as earlier. We were both lost in thought.

He pulled up in front of my house, and I turned to him. "Thank you for the sandwich. And I am on your side, and I support our military. But I need to do what I can to find my dad. Can you understand that?"

Mason nodded. "I'll talk to you later?"

I smiled. "Yes, later."

I went into the house and put the leftover sandwich in the fridge. Trig or Penn would eat it.

Once in the privacy of my room, I checked the message from Luca.

What are you doing tomorrow?

That was it. No hello or pleasantries.

Not sure. Why?

The reply dots showed up immediately.

Want to go see Hurricane Goliath?

What do you mean?

I mean, up close. We can take the bullet train to Nashville, and then the Storm Chasers have a way to get us there.

My heart pounded. I had only seen the footage on the weather app. No one traveled to that part of the country any more. We never even considered it.

But I wanted to see what Dad had seen. Could this really happen?

What time?

8:00, at Union Station.

In the morning?

Ha ha, yes. It's not as cool to see at night.

I thought for a moment. Mom was helping Mella tomorrow at her new place, and the boys wouldn't care where I was. If I were home for dinner, then no one would ask questions.

I'll be there.

Great! I'll be the one in the black shirt.

As if you own anything else.

Guilt curled in my belly as I put the com down. Was I going on a date with someone else? No way. I was going to get more information about what happened to Dad. In fact, I bet Mella would approve. She would say that if I saw it up close, then I'd understand how Dad most likely died in the storm.

I wasn't sure I'd be able to sleep. Tomorrow would either answer my questions, or give me a bunch of new ones. But I needed to see it for myself.

CHAPTER 16

I LEFT MY CAR and my com at the library. I told Mom I was getting an early start on finishing my project and that I'd be there all day. If anyone were to track me, they'd think I was there. I paired a clunky smart watch to my com so I could answer texts if I needed to, without them seeing where I was going. I had Mom's blessing to go to Storm Chaser rallies, but there was no way I'd have her blessing to leave the state. But I had to go.

The walk to the light rail station took longer than I thought, so I was about ten minutes late reaching Union Station. I hoped I hadn't ruined the day.

Luca was easy to spot, even in the busy station. He had parked himself just past security with two coffee cups in his hand. He rolled his eyes at me when I finally made it through the metal detectors.

"I thought you were going to stand me up, Booker." He handed me one cup.

I opened the lid and sniffed. It smelled like a super sweet mocha. Fruity, maybe. Raspberry? "Sorry. It was a long hike to the light rail station from the library. Am I too late? Also, is this almond milk?"

Luca raised an eyebrow, and I could tell he was trying to suppress a grin. "Yes, it's almond milk. I know enough about girls to know that none of you ever consume cow's milk. Unless it's in the form of ice cream. And no, you're not too late, but now we have to hustle."

I laughed and took a sip. "Is this a raspberry mocha?"

"Drink and walk, Booker. Our train leaves in ten minutes, and we need to board, like, now." Luca took off, and I had to jog to keep up with him. Our platform was, of course, the very last one.

The train was pretty empty, which surprised me. I guess it shouldn't have. The government created the Forbidden Zone as a barrier to keep people away from the hurricane, and Nashville was the last major city on its edge. The weather got worse the further south you went from Nashville. The entire states of Alabama, Georgia, and South Carolina had been evacuated decades ago. Even the city of Nashville was dying out, as people migrated north and west, away from the hurricane. Luca and I took two seats in the middle of the train.

I took another sip of my now-cooled coffee. "I have a confession. I have never been east before."

Luca turned to face me. "Are you serious?"

I nodded. "We don't leave Colorado much. Most vacations were spent visiting my grandparents on the Western slope. We went to California once, but nowhere near the coast. We had no reason to go east."

He leaned back as the train pulled away from the station. "I've been East a thousand times. You'll see."

"I'll see what?"

He grinned. "We have about three hours before this train gets to Nashville. That gives you plenty of time to tell me why you were at the library before coming to the station. Were they even open?"

I braced myself as the train shot forward, reaching its top traveling speed of four hundred miles per hour. "I left my car and my com at the library, because I told my family that's where I'd be all day, finishing my senior project."

"They don't know you left the state? What if they try to text you?"

I held up my arm. "I paired this smartwatch with my com. I'll get texts, and I can text back. I just won't be able to video chat with them, so hopefully they won't try. Or if they do, they'll text and ask why, and I'll come up with a reason I can't at the moment."

Luca tipped his cup up, drinking the last of his coffee, then settled back against the window so he could face me. "I take it they don't approve of the Storm Chasers."

I let out a breathy laugh. "My sister, Mella, told me I was betraying the family by even going to the meetings. You know, since my dad worked for USHA and my mom still does."

"I guess I can see that. I mean, my dad would probably disown me if I told him I wanted to work for USHA or something."

"Mom said I should check out the Storm Chasers, but only because she thinks I'll finally see that they don't have the answers I need." I fiddled with the lid on my cup. "And now my mom is dating Chip Sinclair. Do you know who that is?"

He sat up straight. "Uh, yeah. Head of USHA. Are you joking? She's dating the head of USHA?"

I rolled my eyes and nodded. "Chip has been friends with my parents since college. I guess they all started working at USHA right after. And now that Dad has been gone ten years, Chip decided to swoop in and make a play for my mom. And Mom has given up on Dad, so she finally agreed to it."

"Oh my gosh."

"The worst part is, I had gone to my mom's office a few weeks ago and overheard Chip saying some disgusting things about my mom. Like, how he wanted to 'handle' her, and how he's been waiting for years for this. It sounded like he's wanted my mom ever since the college days, but my dad stood in the way."

Luca let out a low whistle. "This is all starting to make sense. I mean, why suddenly you started showing up at the Storm Chasers meetings."

I nodded and handed my empty cup to the attendant who walked by collecting the trash. "Well, I showed up because I just learned about the Storm Chasers. I had never heard of you guys until a few weeks ago. But I felt like I needed to do everything I can to find Dad now. I mean, if I don't find him, Mom will probably end up marrying Chip, and he's so gross."

"Not to mention, your mom shouldn't marry Chip because your dad is still alive."

A lump suddenly formed in my throat, and I looked away, trying to blink back the tears that were threatening to streak my makeup.

He placed a hand on my arm. "Hey, are you okay?"

I took a minute to compose myself, then nodded. "Sorry. It's just you are the first person ever to use words that say my dad is still alive. Everyone, and I mean everyone, keeps telling me to move on. It's so hard to hear my family talk like that. My friends don't say it, but they don't believe like I do that he's still alive. And then there's Mason."

"Yeah, what's up with you and that guy?"

I sighed. "I've liked Mason for forever. Like, since freshman year. We've been in the same group of friends and hung out together whenever we could. But his mom won't let him date. He can't date anyone, not just me. Then this year he finally told me how much he liked me. And I like him back. So as of a few months ago, we became unofficial official boyfriend and girlfriend. We can't be official, because his mom would freak out and ground him for life or something."

"Are you being serious? Aren't you eighteen? Is he?"

"Yeah. It's complicated. Anyway, we had planned to go to Eckman University together. Only the day I got my acceptance letter, Mason told me he got into the Air Force Academy. Which means he had been working on that application and entrance for months, without telling me."

Realization appeared on Luca's face. "Ah. Now it makes sense why he was angry at the Storm Chasers. I know we don't always have nice things to say about the military."

"Exactly."

"Man, your life is nuts."

I let out a laugh. Then I shifted uncomfortably in my seat. "Tell me about it. No, tell me about how you and your dad became so entrenched in the Storm Chasers. Are you still in school?"

"Nah, I graduated early from online school. My dad and I live in an RV at a campground near Cherry Creek Reservoir.

We earn some money providing security for the owners of Park Meadows Mall, and all we need is enough to pay for our camping spot and the food we eat."

My mouth dropped open. "You're homeless?"

"No." An amused grin stretched across his face. "An RV is a home. Just one that can move around."

I was having a hard time wrapping my mind around this. I had never met anyone who didn't live in a house. "What about your mom?"

"She's in Canada. Just outside the Vancouver area, about thirty minutes north of the US border."

My heart squeezed. "Oh. How old were you when your parents got divorced?"

Luca grinned. "They're not divorced. My mom just lives in Canada. She's lived up there since I was ten. She hates the way the US government is handling the storm so much that she defected to Canada. It took her a few years, but she was able to get a work visa and now works at a hospital."

"Why don't you live with her?"

"It's too expensive up there. Mom and Dad gave me the choice, and I chose Dad so I could travel around with the Storm Chasers. We visit her a few times a year. It's cool. My parents still love each other, and they do their own thing."

I narrowed my eyes, taking it all in. "Okay, but how did your dad become a big-wig with the Storm Chasers? I get why Silas is, because of his brother. But how did your dad get involved?"

"My dad and Silas were college roommates. As you know, the Storm Chasers didn't form until after your dad went missing. My dad was working for the U.S. Weather Service in Boulder, and Silas kept calling him with questions about historical hurricane behavior. When Dad realized what was going on, he quit his job and signed on with the Storm Chasers. That's when Mom moved to Canada, and Dad and I hit the road."

I braced myself as the train began its slowdown and stared out the window at the dense, tree-covered hills. It was lush and green here; so different from the crusty brown of Colorado in the early spring. Trees in Colorado didn't get their leaves until late April or early May, and these trees all seemed to be fully ready for summer.

I wondered if I should believe Luca or not. But why would he lie? I suppose if he were to lie, he'd say that he has a normal life, where he lives in a house and his mom is at home making him dinner. I mean, who could dream up living in an RV while your mom lives in a different country?

I felt his eyes on me and I couldn't stop my face from heating. "What?"

He tipped his mouth up into what I figured was his signature half-grin. "Just wondering if I passed whatever test you have."

I snorted. "Aren't I the one supposed to be passing a test? That's what your dad said, right? I'm supposed to be vetted?"

He rolled his eyes. "Yeah, but he forgets everyone is allowed to vet us right back. Yes, we're checking into you. But only a smart person would check us out, too."

"So, is this trip a test?"

Luca stood as soon as the train pulled to a complete stop. "Kind of. Time always tells, doesn't it? But mostly, I thought you'd want to see the storm."

My stomach went on the rollercoaster ride that it usually only reserved for talk of my dad. I had almost forgotten the whole reason we were on this trip. I was finally going to get to see Hurricane Goliath up close.

I jumped up and stepped back so Luca could lead the way. "I do want to see it."

"Then right this way, Booker. We're almost there."

CHAPTER 17

Nothing could have surprised me more than Luca walking right up to a car in the Nashville train station parking lot and getting in the driver's seat.

He got back out when I just stood and stared. "Come on, Booker. We're kind of in a time crunch here."

"Whose car is this?"

"It belongs to the Storm Chasers. We leave it here to get us to and from headquarters. We can't take the light rail, because our headquarters are on the outskirts of town."

I got in the front seat, and Luca set the destination in the autopilot. He leaned back as the car drove us away from the station.

The sky was a mixture of sun and clouds. It looked like a storm was building toward the south. Towering cumulonimbus clouds formed a wall in the distance.

I couldn't tear my eyes away from the clouds. "Is that it?"

"Sort of. It's the northern-most edge. The weather is quite unstable south of Nashville, which is why they evacuated Alabama. But we're still about 100 miles away from the edge of the hurricane."

It took about thirty minutes to get to the Storm Chasers' headquarters once the car hit hyper-drive on the edge of the city. Luca wasn't kidding when he said it was on the outskirts of town. The last building we had passed was about ten miles back.

The headquarters were an abandoned farm, complete with several large sheds. No cars parked on the dirt patch in front of the neglected farmhouse.

I swallowed. "Where is everyone?"

"In Washington, D.C., remember? The vote? You helped get funding and volunteers for the whole thing?"

I let out a nervous laugh. "Oh yeah. I forgot about it."

Luca powered down the car and turned toward me. "To be honest, I only brought you here because everyone is gone. You're not cleared yet, and I'd be in trouble. But I know you need to make up your mind about us, and I think this will help."

I gave him a sideways glance. "The thing I care about most is finding my dad. Not the Storm Chasers' cause."

He smiled. "That's fair. Come on."

We got out of the car, but instead of heading to the house, Luca led the way to the nearest shed. The shed was a giant metal structure, bigger than the house. An acrid scent caught me off guard.

"What is that?" I asked, sniffing the air.

"What is what?"

"That smell. It's like a city or something. I thought the country would smell like grass and cows, but that chemical is strong."

He used his key card to unlock the giant sliding door on the front of the shed. "It's gas."

"Gas? What uses gas out here?"

"Come help me. This door needs two people to push."

I pushed on the edge while Luca pulled hard on the handle. I stopped short once it was open.

"That uses gas."

Inside was a small airplane. I couldn't believe it. Authorities banned air travel twenty years ago because of the unstable atmosphere. The bullet train system proved to be a faster, safer, and cleaner way to travel, anyway. Air travel was only allowed out of New York and Seattle, because travel over the northern oceans was the safest, and you couldn't take a train to London or Tokyo yet. Although I had heard they were working on bullet ocean liners.

"We're going in that?"

Luca marched to the plane. "You wanted to see Goliath up close, right? Nothing is closer than the sky."

I hurried after him. "How on earth can we? You can't hide a plane in the sky. Won't they shoot us down or something?"

He laughed. "You watch too many movies. No, they won't shoot us down. They don't monitor air travel anymore because they banned it, you know. The Storm Chasers do this all the time. No one is even looking for planes, especially not ones this small."

"But someone could see us."

"We always fly south. No one is between us and the Forbidden Zone. Trust me, no one will see us." He grabbed a clipboard hanging on the wall near the door and jogged back to the plane.

"What are you doing?"

"Pre-flight check."

"So you've done this before?"

"Twice. I mean, I've flown it twice by myself now. I've been on an air mission eight times."

"What are the air missions for?"

Luca stopped and looked at me. "We're looking for ways into the storm. Safe points of entry. Plus, there's something else we're monitoring. Now, you've got to put a sock in it, Booker. I have to concentrate on this pre-flight check. Safety first, you know."

I followed him around the plane as he touched various things and made notes on the clipboard. Air travel baffled me. Even this small plane looked too heavy to get into the air. My trailing behind must have annoyed him, because he opened one door and told me to climb in.

The plane had four seats, two in front, and two behind. I settled into what I assumed was the passenger side and stared at all the knobs and gauges on the panel.

Luca climbed into the seat next to mine. He handed me a pair of headphones.

"Put these on so we can talk to each other in the air. It gets a little loud."

He put his on, then pushed a few buttons on the panel. The engine roared alive, louder than anything I'd ever heard. I placed the headphones on, and the roar immediately became dampened.

He grinned. "Good job, Booker. Way to follow directions. Now, buckle up."

I snapped my buckle in place as he drove the plane toward the barn door. My heart raced and my stomach twisted.

"Is this safe? This is a bad idea. Maybe we shouldn't be doing this."

He shot me a glance, then turned his focus back to what he was doing. "Don't chicken out. It's safe, and it's fine. Also, it's the fastest way to get there."

I took a deep breath as he drove onto a straight, well-maintained country road. With a few more switches, Luca pressed a few pedals, and we sped forward. Within seconds, we had lifted into the air. I squeezed my eyes shut and held onto my seatbelt for dear life.

"Booker. Open your eyes."

We were higher than any building I had ever been in. Despite the slight rattle to the plane and low drone of the engines, the ride was quite smooth. I stared at the ground rushing below us, and a flood of adrenaline filled my veins.

"No, not at that." Luca pointed out the front window. "That."

The wall of clouds loomed even higher than I had thought they were from the ground. They stretched in either direction as far as I could see. The clouds seemed to roll and churn, as if they wanted to escape, but something held them back.

He headed straight for the clouds for about fifteen minutes. Neither of us spoke. Luca focused on flying the plane, while I was mesmerized by both the clouds and our high altitude above the ground. I jumped when I heard his voice in the headphones. "Now look down."

I gasped. We had been racing over the green hills and trees, but suddenly everything was flattened and brown. A clear line separated the green from the brown, as if someone had marked a boundary. One side was alive and thriving, the other side looked like a giant boot had stamped it down. I had seen pictures of damage like this before, but they were all pictures of the aftermath of F5 tornados that ravaged eastern Colorado and western Kansas every summer.

"What happened here?"

Luca turned the plane, flying us above the line, which ran east to west. "Hurricanes spawn tornadoes. But doesn't this look intentional to you? Like someone designed it that way?"

"Designed?"

"I mean, the line is too straight. It doesn't go beyond this point. It's like the tornadoes had a border they couldn't cross, so they ran alongside their fence, looking for a place to push past it."

"You make it sound like they're alive."

"Don't the clouds look like they are hitting a wall?"

"Yeah, I noticed that, but what does that mean?"

Luca swung the plane back toward the wall of clouds. "We think it means someone created a border to block the storm. The damage you see on the ground is decades old. The first tornadoes to make that line happened right after Hurricane Goliath showed up. But the Storm Chasers have monitored this border for about five years now, and tornadoes show up like clockwork every three months to reinforce the line."

"Are you kidding me?"

Suddenly, the plane lurched and dropped a short distance. I shrieked and grabbed a handle next to the door. Luca swore and gripped the controls. The plane seemed to dance all over the place, as if it wanted to get to the ground and it was going to fight Luca until it got there.

"What's happening?" I cried.

He grunted as he pulled back on the control stick. "I don't know. It might be the wind, or–"

The plane tipped, and I found myself pressed against my door, with my gaze fixed on the ground. The coffee Luca had bought me threatened to come back up. He pulled and got the plane level again.

"I've got to land. Hang on."

My eyes were glued open as we raced toward the ground faster than I imagined was safe. But how was I supposed to know? Was this normal for air travel? Maybe this is why they banned small planes. I couldn't believe how stupid I had been. No one, not even Dasha, had any idea where I was. And I didn't even kiss Mason goodbye last night. I never had a chance to tell Mom what Chip said. And...

And then we were on the ground. The plane bounced twice, then skidded to a stop in the wide brown field. How Luca had seen the road to land on, I'll never know. I took a deep breath in through my nose and slowly let it out through my mouth as he flipped switches and turned knobs, killing the engine.

He tore off his headphones, then put a gentle hand on my arm. I stared at him with wide eyes, and he gently took my headphones off my head.

His eyes searched mine. "Are you okay?"

I swallowed, unable to tear my eyes away from his. "Yeah. I think so."

He held my gaze for a second longer, then reached for his door handle. "Come on. Let's get out."

I fumbled for my door handle, but Luca was the one to open it from the outside. A small grin appeared on his face.

"Seat belt, Booker. You'll want to unclasp it if you want to get out."

I unbuckled, then grabbed Luca's outstretched hand, and he helped me out of the plane. We walked a few yards away from the offending vehicle and sat on an overturned log. It was really windy, and my first thought was I wished I had a jacket.

It took a few minutes before I could speak. "What happened?"

"Uh, we almost ran out of fuel." Luca ran his hand through his hair. "I promise I checked it twice like I'm supposed to, but I miscalculated how much I needed. I have never been this far before."

"You told me you had been on eight missions!"

"Yeah, I have, but not this far. We never go this far into the Damage Zone. The wind killed my gas mileage."

I wrapped my arms around myself and looked around. There was no place to hide from the wind. "Do we have to walk back?"

He shook his head. "Just hang on." He pulled out his com, hit a few buttons, and within seconds Miri Day's face appeared on the screen.

"Sup. Whoa. Where are you?" Her face got close to her camera, as if that could make her see better.

He held his com up, so the camera faced our surroundings.

"Luca! You went into the Damage Zone? By yourself?"

He turned the com back to him. "Not alone. Ashlyn Booker is here." He turned the camera to me, and I gave a stupid wave.

Miri's jaw dropped. "What do you think you're doing?"

"I wanted to show her. We ran out of gas and I had to land. Can you track me? And can you bring me more fuel?"

"Are you kidding me?"

"No, I'm not! The crew on duty will be back at the Nashville headquarters tomorrow morning, and I have to have the plane back so I can clean it, and then Ashlyn and I have to get back to Denver by tonight."

Miri rolled her eyes. "Yes, I can save your butt. It'll take me a few hours to get there, though."

Luca swallowed. "Yeah. But hurry. Because you know what day it is."

Miri's eyes got wide. "Oh my gosh. I'm on my way." The screen went dark.

I grabbed Luca's arm. "I have questions."

"Shoot."

"First, is Miri, like, in Nashville? Because if she's still in Denver, it will take more than a few hours for her to get out here. Second, how will she get here? I didn't see another plane. And third, what day is it?"

He sighed. "Yes, Miri is in Nashville. It's Storm Chaser policy to never travel to headquarters alone, and Miri was going to meet me there later today. I didn't tell her why we couldn't travel together, but she doesn't ask a lot of questions. She's cool like that."

I wasn't sure how to feel about Luca not telling Miri that I was coming. But I guess I didn't tell anyone in my family that I was coming with Luca, so who was I to judge?

"And how will she get out here?"

"There's a second plane in the other shed."

"And what day is it?"

Luca paused. "It's going to be fine, okay?"

"What do you mean?"

He got up and paced away. "Remember when I said tornadoes reinforce the border every three months?"

Chills ran up my back, and not from the wind. "Is today the three-month mark?"

He nodded. "Today or tomorrow. We haven't quite figured out the exact timing, but we know they will happen soon."

"Luca. There's no shelter out here."

He came back and sat down beside me. "I really think we'll be fine. The clouds are still stuck behind their wall. Miri will make it. I'm sure."

I stared at the sky. I could only hope he was right.

CHAPTER 18

LUCA PACED AROUND THE outside of the plane, talking to himself. If I had had my com, I would have taken a video of him from the safety of inside the plane to show him how dumb he looked.

The plane lurched as a giant gust of wind slammed against it. We were the only thing taller than three feet for miles, and the wind seemed to be on a personal mission to make us as flat as everything around us.

I knew we were in danger, but I couldn't help but laugh when a gust almost knocked Luca over. He recovered from his stumble, then jogged back to the plane, wrenching the door open.

"Was it worth it?" I asked as soon as he pulled his door shut.

He gave me a side glance. "Yes. This footage will be priceless."

"Because none of you have ever come this far in?"

"Right. We've only taken pictures of the edge. Man, this wind. I hope Miri can make it."

My stomach felt rock hard. I was trying my hardest to stay cool about all of this, but I wasn't sure how much longer I could keep it together. The cloud wall had shifted in the last hour and now seemed to ooze toward us. The fluffy white towers had turned a sickly gray.

"Can you track her?"

Luca pulled out his com. "Ah, there she is." He hopped out and started waving his arms.

I jumped out and ran to his side. "I think she can see us. We're the only thing out here."

Miri landed her plane with ease. She killed her engine and jumped out. "You gotta work with the wind, Luca," she yelled.

A crack of thunder made us all jump.

"I think those clouds are darker," I said. "And...greener."

Miri's eyes got wide. "We gotta go. Come on." She wrenched open the side door of her plane and put two huge gas cans on the ground.

"Booker, grab a can. It'll take eight of these to get us enough fuel to get back." Luca grabbed one and headed back toward our plane.

The gas can was much heavier than it looked. I struggled to lift it as Miri plunked two more on the ground. "You flew with open gas in your plane?"

Miri smirked. "Not the first time. It's what we do. Come on, we gotta hustle."

Filling the gas tank took longer than I hoped. The only real help I was able to give was hauling back the much lighter, empty cans back to Miri's plane and tucking them in the back of the cargo area. The first raindrops hit us just as we had finished.

"You good?" Miri shouted over the wind.

Luca gave a thumbs up. "Yeah! Go. We're right behind you."

She raced back to her plane and had her engine on before I had buckled my seatbelt. Luca and I shoved our headsets on and he started flipping switches.

"Uh, Luca." I grabbed his arm. He paused and looked out the window.

A slender, snake-like funnel cloud raced from the sky to the ground in the distance. Luca pressed a button that fired up the engine. "We'll be in the air in two minutes. Just hang on."

It was impossible to look away from the tornado. As Luca began moving the plane, two more funnels fell from the sky close to the first one. He swung the plane around and coaxed it up to speed. I twisted around, trying to keep my eyes on the funnels. The three of them appeared stationary, waiting for the signal to attack. I understood tornados well enough to realize that when they looked motionless, they were actually heading straight for us.

Luca let out a laugh as soon as we were airborne. "This wind is actually helping us. It's pushing us from behind. I bet we'll hardly use any of Miri's gas getting back."

We didn't speak at all during the flight back to headquarters. Luca appeared upset, and the sight of those three funnels haunted me. I didn't know him well enough to feel like I could talk about my fear, or to ask him if he was alright.

Miri had arrived before us and opened the barn's back door, allowing Luca to drive straight in. As soon as he cut the engine, I jumped out and stopped myself from doing something dumb, like kissing the ground. I never wanted to fly again.

She jogged over to me. "Are you okay? Did you see those funnels?"

I swallowed and nodded. "I can't believe it."

"Did you get a picture of them, Luca?"

He groaned. "No. I didn't even think about it. I was too busy trying to get the plane off the ground."

My mouth dropped open. "That's what you're worried about? Not getting pictures?"

He rubbed the back of his neck. "I can't hide that I took the plane. Everyone will see the mileage and notice the missing gas. Which means my dad is going to find out. And I know he won't be happy that I did this, but I thought getting the footage inside the Disaster Zone might smooth things over. Pictures of the funnels would have made this worth it."

Miri grabbed his arm. "It'll be okay. I'll vouch, and so will Ashlyn. Three witnesses should be enough."

"And you have the footage you took while we were waiting for Miri." I don't know why I was helping. I wanted to be mad at him for risking my life.

A gust of wind slammed against the shed, the metal howling in protest. I let out an involuntary shriek. Even Luca looked rattled.

"Did those funnels follow us?" I asked.

Luca shook his head. "No, but the storms around here are wicked. This is why people don't live here anymore."

"Why don't you guys get going? The last train to Denver leaves in an hour, and you'll have to leave now if you're going to make it. I'll take care of the planes and bunk in the farmhouse. I'll slip out on the first train tomorrow." Miri gently pushed us toward the barn door.

Luca looked relieved. "Thanks, Miri."

I stopped. "Seriously, thank you. You saved our lives."

She rolled her eyes, but she was grinning. "So dramatic. But yeah, I did. And I won't forget it either."

I laughed, then ran and jumped in the car. "I like her."

Luca nodded. "She's a good egg. And she always comes through. She's gotten me out of quite a few scrapes."

"How long have you known her?"

"Since Dad and I started living in the RV. She and her family were on vacation in the RV park where we first stayed, and back then Dad and I told every single person we met about the Storm Chasers. Her family was the first one to take us seriously. They've been part of the Storm Chasers ever since."

The adrenaline pumping through my veins made me hyper aware of the storm clouds chasing us back to Nashville. And then I realized something.

"Hey." I glared at Luca. "You said you were taking me to see Goliath, not some dumb field."

Luca's mouth tipped up. "Goliath is more than just the swirling storm. I showed you what Goliath is doing, didn't I? And that's as close as we can get."

I turned to the window to hide my hot cheeks. How dumb was I to think I'd see the actual rotating storm? Luca said we were going to Nashville, not to space, which would be the only place we could get a bird's eye view.

We barely made it to the train on time. The adrenaline crashed as soon as I sank into my seat, and I was starving. I hadn't had anything but the coffee Luca had brought me that morning. I leaned my head back and closed my eyes, trying to ignore the growling in my stomach. But Luca spoke just before I fell asleep.

"There's a big mission coming up. I think you'd be great for it. Do you want in?"

"What's the mission?" I didn't even open my eyes.

"I don't have all the details. We never do until the mission planning meeting, because if someone isn't going to be a part of it, they don't need to know. Plausible deniability and all that."

That sounded super sketchy. "Then how would I know if I want in?"

Luca pulled out his com and opened a picture of the Disaster Zone. "That's how. How could you not after what you've just seen? Have you ever seen this before?"

I shook my head.

"Of course not. Because they don't show this part on the news. Or tell anyone that they use tornadoes to guard the border of the hurricane. Something is going on, and we have to dig out the truth to show the world."

I sat back in my seat and stared out the window. My smart watch buzzed with a text from Mom asking if I wanted her to make me some dinner. I typed out that I would be a few hours still, and that she didn't have to worry about me. She sent a kissy face emoji.

For a moment, I wished I could go back a few weeks. Before my birthday, before Chip started pushing his way into our family, before my sister and brothers said they were going to move on with their lives. Life back then was so peaceful. I was so full of hope about graduating and going to college with Mason.

Everything had changed so quickly. Even my plans with Mason fell apart. And now I had learned enough about the hurricane that I had so many questions that I had never even known to ask. Questions that fanned the flame of hope that my dad was truly alive.

I couldn't live with the questions anymore. I had to find out the answers. The Storm Chasers mission might offer some answers.

"When is the meeting?"

Luca's eyes lit up. "Tomorrow. 9:00 am. I'll text you the location in the morning, if you're in. They never give us the location until an hour before."

I took a deep breath. "I'm in."

Chapter 19

Mom was sitting at the kitchen table entranced by something on her com when I walked into the house after nine o'clock that night.

"Did you get your project done?" She didn't even look up.

"Yeah." I paused in the kitchen's doorway. "I'm not feeling that great. I might be coming down with a cold. So I'm going to stay home from church tomorrow, okay? I'll sleep in."

That made her put down her com. "What are your symptoms? What do you need?"

"Nothing. I mean, I don't need anything. Just rest, I think. I'm exhausted, and my throat is a little scratchy." The thing about my throat was a lie.

She left the table and grabbed a small glass out of the cabinet. "Come gargle salt water before you go to bed."

I groaned. Mom thought salt water was the magic remedy for all ailments. I would never admit to her that gargling salt water did help when I had a sore throat. But now I had to take her nasty concoction, even though I didn't need one. But I guessed it was a small price to pay for the lie I told.

I gargled the warm water, spitting into the sink. She made me repeat the process until I gagged. "Okay, thanks Mom. That's enough. I'm going to bed now."

She brushed the hair out of my eyes, then pulled my head toward her and pressed her lips to my forehead. "Good, no fever. Sleep as long as you can tomorrow. I'm going to meet Chip for lunch after church, so I'll be back in the afternoon."

I scowled. "He's not going to church with you?"

Mom gave me a look. "We haven't gotten to where we've talked about whose church we'd go to yet. Are you saying you're ready for me to invite him to ours?"

A wave of relief washed over me. I wanted this phase of their relationship to last as long as possible. Or at least until I found Dad. "No, you're right. Okay, fine. Goodnight."

She pulled me back into a hug. "Feel better, Mini-Muffin. Text me if you want me to get you some medicine, okay?"

I stopped and wrapped my arms around her. She was the best mom on the planet, and for a minute I almost spilled everything that I had seen, and was planning to do. But there wasn't enough evidence yet.

I woke early the next morning, but had to stay in bed while my family went to church. Hanging out in bed is one of my favorite things, but I was so antsy about the meeting that lying around for an extra hour was torture. Finally, the door slammed one last time. I popped out of bed and headed to the shower.

Luca left me a text while I showered. I typed the address into the map app, my stomach dropping when I saw it was a storage unit in an older part of town.

I can't drive there. Can you come get me?

What do you mean?

> There are no light rail stations nearby. I have to leave my car here, so my family thinks I'm still in bed. I need a ride.

> Oh. Maybe. Where do you live?

I texted him my address, then stood in front of my closet. What was someone supposed to wear to a secret mission planning meeting?

> I can come get you, if you can be ready in 10 minutes.

I groaned. I hadn't even dried my hair.

> Yes, I'll be ready.

> Cool. See you in 10.

I threw on jeans and a t-shirt, and hurried to put on makeup. I could do with wet, messy hair, but not without eyeliner and mascara. I turned the tracker off on my com and slipped it into my bag. Almost getting sucked up by three tornados taught me I always want to be able to contact my family. But they didn't need to know where I was. I rushed downstairs to grab coffee, then grabbed some energy bars. No way I was going to repeat yesterday's adventure without food.

I flew out the door and ran to the entrance of my cul-de-sac, just as Luca was driving toward it. He had barely stopped when I hopped in the side.

"What? You didn't want me to see where you lived?"

I shook my head, trying to slow my breathing from my jog. "No, I didn't want my nosy neighbors to see me getting into your car. They'd tell my mom, or worse, my brothers."

He smiled. "You're really getting into the Spy Life, aren't you Booker?"

I peppered him with questions about the mission during the drive to the meeting place. I couldn't believe he knew nothing about it, but he wasn't budging. Either he was very good at keeping secrets, or he really didn't know anything.

Luca punched in the code to get in through the gate of the storage facility, and we drove to the very back of the property. If I hadn't been with him, I would have chickened out. No smart girl would ever go to a place like this by herself.

We parked behind a row of four cars, then walked into the building that housed the units. It was creepier than I had imagined. The hall was dimly lit, and the row of units made me feel closed in, with no hope of escape.

I stayed a step behind Luca as we turned two corners, then stopped in front of one of the units. Luca tapped on the door three times, and the door rolled up.

The unit was bare. Eight people sat in folding chairs in a U-shape facing an old-fashioned whiteboard, the kind that you drew on with markers. I immediately felt better when I saw Miri. She gave a little wave.

Tyler Denzio scowled when he saw me. "What is she doing here?"

Luca swallowed. "She wants in, Dad."

"She hasn't been vetted!"

Miri raised her hand. "I'll vouch for her."

I was getting tired of hearing about this whole "vetting" process. I clenched my fists and took a step forward. "What does that even mean? Being vetted? What do you want? My criminal record? I don't have one. My birth certificate, to prove that Jonah Booker is my dad? I guess I can bring you that, but if I do, you have to show me yours."

The other people in the chairs broke into laughter.

"Come on, Tyler," said a bald man wearing a tight T-shirt. "We don't vet kids like we do adults."

Tyler shot the man a glare. "Remember what happened the last time we let a stranger in the mission planning meeting?"

I took a deep breath as I tried to think before I spoke. "Look, I don't know what happened, but I can tell you I'm good, or cool, or whatever. I just want to find my dad. And I've seen the Disaster Zone and the guard dog tornadoes, and I'm a ready, willing, capable body for whatever this mission is."

Tyler's eyes grew wide. "When did you see the Disaster Zone?"

Luca spoke up. "Yesterday. I took her out on the plane. And I, uh, ran out of gas, so Miri had to bring me some. And just before we could take off to fly back to headquarters, we saw three funnel clouds drop out of the sky. On schedule, Dad! Just like we thought."

Tyler's mouth opened and closed. He folded his arms and didn't say anything.

Silas Chapman stood up and stepped forward. "We haven't met, but my brother knew your dad. I'm Silas." He held out his hand.

I shook it. "Yeah, Luca told me. It's nice to meet you."

He turned around and clapped Tyler on the shoulder. "There. Vetted. Now, uh, you can have my chair. I'll stand." He took his place next to the whiteboard.

The other people were much nicer than Tyler. The group consisted of two men, two women, and one other teen, a kid named Jack Farmer. Jack looked like he was twelve, but insisted he was sixteen. The fact that one more teen was there silenced all the fears I had that this group was going to kidnap me or something.

Tyler gave a final grunt, then turned to the whiteboard, making notes as he went along.

"Here's the mission: we're going to raid the main USHA facility to get the info we need to infiltrate the storm."

I gasped, but everyone else nodded like they already knew what the mission was. "But how?"

Tyler rolled his eyes. "This is why I didn't want any newbies. Do I really have to explain this all again?"

Luca clenched his fists. "Dad, come on."

Silas put a hand on Tyler's shoulder, which seemed to calm him down. "I have contacts inside the storm."

I couldn't believe what I was hearing. "How do you communicate with them? Why didn't you bring this up during the meetings?"

"They are only fifty miles in. There are shelters made of concrete, and we have radios that can make it that far. However, communications only go that far. For now."

Despite his face being locked into a permanent scowl, Tyler managed to scowl even more. "And we don't discuss it in meetings because not everyone has gone through the vetting process."

I rolled my eyes. If Trig wanted to play a drinking game, he should have taken a drink every time Tyler said the stupid word "vetted."

Ginger, a woman who seemed to be around Mom's age, stood and passed out papers to the group. I must have looked surprised, because she winked at me. "We can destroy paper. People can track digital files. I used to work with Tyler at the US National Weather Service office. In fact, I was his boss, so I'm a better meteorologist than him." Everyone laughed again, and Silas punched Tyler in the arm. Tyler gave a ghost of a smile. "After monitoring the storm for ten years, I have seen distinct patterns on the radar. We can use that radar to chart a path, but we need a couple more pieces of tech to finish the chart." The paper listed a series of coordinates with dates next to them. The first date was in three weeks.

Willie, the bald man, piped in. "The tech we need is in USHA. They have tech pads that sync with the satellites that tell the actual truth about the storm. We just want to grab one."

"More than one," the other woman said. "We need at least four. We need two dedicated to the radar, and two dedicated to getting past the dang military blockades."

Tyler held up his hand. "Don't get greedy, Sybil. Four would be great, but the mission is one. If we get one, we can get out. If we can grab four, then we will. We only need one to consider the mission a success."

Hugh, a small, wiry man with bright blue eyes, leaned forward. "Ashlyn, have you seen the news that talks about the weak spot in Goliath?"

"Yeah, but that was over two weeks ago, on my birthday."

He shook his head. "That was just the start of it. Once every ten years, the storm loses strength for a couple of months. The untrained public wouldn't know the difference, but it's a significant weakening. They no longer mention it in the news, but they lower Goliath's classification from a Category 5 to a Category 3 during this weakening. And the peak happens in four weeks."

Silas jumped in. "That's why we need to raid USHA on Friday night. We need those pads so we can plan the next phase, which is entering the storm."

I sat back in my chair and shook my head. "You can't get into USHA. Have you ever been? There's security everywhere. I mean, it's not like you can just walk through the front doors."

Jack piped in. "There are side doors."

It had been ages since Luca last spoke up, but he finally did. "There's one more reason we need Ashlyn on this team." I had no idea what he was talking about.

He sat up straighter and smiled at his dad. "Ashlyn's mom works at USHA. She's the head of Production and Export. And she's dating Chip Sinclair."

My stomach rolled when I realized what he was getting at. "Are you kidding me?"

Luca turned to me with pleading eyes. "Booker, we need your mom's access card."

Chapter 20

I RUBBED MY EYES as I leaned against Luca's car. I really needed to make better choices. Letting him drive was the first terrible choice I made today; now I was at his mercy to get me home. Storming outside my second terrible choice. Now I didn't know how much longer this meeting was going to be.

I had just decided to swallow my pride and go back in when Luca and Miri came out the door.

I stood up straight. "I have to go. My mom will be done with church any minute, and she'll want to check on me, and then she'll ask why I turned my tracker off."

Luca nodded. "Yeah, we can go. Is it okay if Miri comes with us?"

Miri was looking at me like I might fly off the handle at any moment. "I want Luca to drop me off at my house after yours, so I don't have to wait on Ginger. They're nerding out over the weather data in there, and that might take all afternoon."

I let out a laugh. "Of course." This was better, actually. Then I didn't need to talk. Or sit by Luca. I climbed into the back seat.

Luca and Miri exchanged glances before getting into the car.

We drove in silence for about five minutes before Luca cleared his throat.

"Um, about the access card."

I crossed my arms. "Do you even understand what you're asking me to do?"

Miri glanced back at me from her seat. "But it's the key to the entire mission. Ha ha, get it? The key?"

Luca shot her a scowl. "Yeah, we get it."

"She'll know I took it. She just gave me this big speech about how we were all adults now and it was time to get to know each other as friends, but I'm still in high school. She could still, like, ground me, or keep me from going to the prom. Or worse, the senior trip."

I wasn't sure I was ready to betray my mom like this. They were asking me to cross a line, and for what? I mean, clearly some shady stuff was going on with the hurricane, but would any of this help me find Dad?

I stared at the back of Luca's head. I couldn't believe I hadn't seen it before. He had only invited me to see the hurricane because of my mom, not my dad. These Storm Chasers didn't care about Dad at all. They just wanted to take down USHA. Even if that meant taking down my mom along with it.

We were close to my cul-de-sac. "Pull over. Here. Drop me here." Luca pulled over, and I fumbled with my seat belt.

"Ashlyn?" Miri was looking at me with hopeful eyes.

"Sure, you can have the card. As soon as you tell me how you're going to betray your family." I jumped out of the car, slammed the door shut, and took off toward my house, not looking back.

As soon as I was back in my room, I crawled into bed. I wanted to cry, but no tears came. Why had I let myself hope that the Storm Chasers could, or would, help me find Dad?

I don't know how long I laid there, buried under my covers, before someone opened my door.

"Ash?" Mom poked her head in my room. "How are you feeling?"

I grunted. "Okay. Better. Still tired."

"Do you want some food? I brought home some French onion soup from Millie's, in case you wanted something."

Warm fuzzies filled my heart. I rolled over. "Yeah, that sounds good. Thanks, Mom. I'll come soon."

Mom came over and pressed her lips to my forehead. "Good. No fever still. You can warm up the soup when you're ready. I asked for croutons on the side and there's also extra cheese. I'm going outside to do some yard work, okay?"

I nodded and tossed back the covers as Mom left the room. I couldn't survive on coffee and energy bars alone. I needed real food.

I prepped the flash cooker and dumped the soup, croutons, and cheese in a bowl. Within seconds, the smell of onions and cheese filled the kitchen, and I felt settled for the first time in weeks. I needed to concentrate on home. I loved my home. I opened the sliding glass door that led from the kitchen to the backyard. It was a beautiful late March day. One of those warm, spring days that made me ready for everything to be in bloom again. It might snow tomorrow, but today was a day for fresh air.

I sat at the kitchen table with my bowl of soup. Just before I took my first bite, I heard Chip's voice in my backyard, and I stopped.

"Want some help?"

"No. I mean, yes. But no." My mom's voice sounded like she was frustrated. Or crying. Or both.

"Why didn't you wait for me? I said I'd be here as soon as I changed my clothes."

"I should be able to do this. Trig and Penn are leaving, and I need to figure out how to do lawn work on my own." She sniffed. "I don't have the stamina. I'm old and out of shape."

It got quiet for a minute, and so I peeked out the kitchen window. Mom stood near the back deck with a rake. A pile of dead grass sat next to her feet. Chip stood next to her, his arm around her shoulder. He kissed the side of her head.

"I told you I'm more than happy to take care of this for you."

"You mean you're more than happy to hire a lawn service."

He chuckled. "Okay, sure. Yes. What's wrong with that?"

Mom shrugged. "Jonah always did the yard work. He taught the boys when they were young, and they took over after he left. We just like to do it ourselves."

Chip was quiet for a moment. "Then I'll learn too. And we can figure it out together. We need a hobby to do together."

Mom wiped her face. "I hate outdoor work."

Chip laughed. "Then I'll hire someone! Don't worry, Liv. We'll figure out a new hobby. But for now, do you want me to order Chinese for dinner? I'll get it for the whole family, or whoever is here tonight. That way, you can concentrate on that meeting for tomorrow and not worry about food. And I know that crab Rangoon can't take away the sorrow of the kids moving out, but maybe good memories together will?"

The look on Chip's face as he gazed into Mom's eyes made my heart squeeze. I had seen that look before. Mason had given me it to me right before our first kiss. Right before every kiss, in fact.

I looked away from the window and returned to my soup. I didn't want to witness my mom getting kissed. Although, something inside me melted. Maybe whatever was happening between my mom and Chip was real.

First time, I truly considered Mom. Mella was right—Mom's husband was gone, her kids were moving out, and even I was moving on to the next phase of my life. Even though Mason and I were in a fight, I still wanted to spend all my time with him. Which meant that I wouldn't be home to spend it with Mom. To be honest, I just assumed Mom worked all the time, but the truth was that I didn't really know what she did when I was out with Mason or Dasha. Was she sitting at home, being lonely? That thought made me sad.

I believed her when she said she supported all we were doing. Which meant that I should support what she wanted to do to move on with her life.

I played around with the last crouton in my soup. It always came back to this question: was it time to let go of Dad? The Storm Chasers thought that the Disaster Zone and the tornados and the radar images all pointed to the fact that people could go into the storm, but maybe all it proved was how deadly the storm was.

"What does Ashlyn like?"

Chip's voice made me drop my spoon in my bowl with a clatter. I grabbed it and winced.

"She's a big fan of lo mein. And orange chicken."

"Good. I'll get all her favorites. That will win her over to Team Chip, right?"

Mom groaned, but I could hear the smile in her voice. "You're not supposed to say that about yourself."

Chip chuckled again. "Oops."

I jumped up and washed out my bowl. I wanted to be upstairs before they came into the house. I could make myself eat dinner with them, but I wasn't ready to just hang out on a Sunday afternoon with Chip.

Had I been wrong about him this whole time? Maybe it was time to give him a chance.

Chapter 21

Sunday's dinner with Chip wasn't so bad. Mostly because Trig and Penn were there to distract everyone with their banter. To my surprise, Chip seemed to sit back and observe. He didn't try to insert himself into anything. I couldn't help but notice the way he always seemed to be touching Mom - his arm across the back of her chair, his thumb stroking her shoulder. But it didn't seem possessive. Just present.

During lunch at school the next day, Mason slid an unopened chocolate pudding cup toward me, his look hesitant. Gretchen and Rosalie were locked in their usual flirt-fest with Jude and Zed, so it was a good time to slip away. I didn't open the pudding, but I nodded toward the door, and Mason and I headed for our usual empty hallway.

I stopped at the end, behind the row of lockers, and kept my gaze on the unopened pudding cup.

He ran his hand down my arm and laced his fingers through mine. "Ash."

I looked up into his eyes. "Um, hey."

"Happy six-monthaversary."

My cheeks heated. I couldn't believe I had forgotten the date.

His mouth tipped up in an amused smile. "Did you forget?"

"No! I mean, I guess. I..." I was fumbling around for words, my cheeks hot.

Mason laughed, and he pulled me into a hug. "Relax. It's okay. I know it's been weird lately, but I'll never forget the day I finally told you how much I liked you, and you didn't laugh or try to turn me down gently."

I tipped my head back to look at his handsome face. "I told you. I've liked you for years."

His eyes dropped to my lips. "I gave you the pudding because we had pudding right before our first kiss."

I pressed a little closer. "I remember."

He glanced down the hall before giving me a quick peck. "Can you go with me after school? I kind of have something planned, but we need to leave right after school ends."

I hesitated. There was a Storm Chaser meeting that evening. But did I even want to go? The Storm Chasers were turning out to be much more dangerous than I had expected. Yes, they had information about the hurricane that I had never heard before, but so far, none of it gave me any leads on Dad.

It was time to grow up. I wanted my peaceful life back, and all the turmoil started when I started going to those dumb rallies. They were just fundraising meetings, anyway. The Storm Chasers needed money to do their protests and whatnot, and I had no money. It was a waste of time.

"Yeah. What do you have planned?"

Mason gave me a second quick kiss, then started walking backward down the hall. "You'll see." He shot me a beaming grin before turning and jogging around the corner.

I didn't hear a thing in my afternoon classes. The mystery of our plans made it difficult to concentrate. I hurried to my locker as soon as the final bell rang and stopped short. A red heart balloon was tied to my lock. I tried to stop myself from smiling as I opened my locker, as if that were a normal occurrence. I untied the balloon and carried it with my bag out the front doors of the school. My com buzzed.

The stone tables by the pickleball court.

I smiled and hurried to the spot where Mason had first told me he liked me. He was sitting on the table with two cups in his hand.

I gasped. "Is that raspberry lemonade boba?"

He nodded. "You freaked out over it when I bought it for you last fall."

I took a long swig from the straw and let two of the popping bubbles into my mouth. I bit down, and the burst of raspberry chased the tang of the lemonade away.

"Thank you."

Mason grabbed my hand. "What time do you have to be home?"

I shrugged. "I mean, I have one essay to do, but it won't take me long. So I guess anytime."

"I have to be home by 7:00. That gives us four hours."

"To do what?"

He grinned. "Come on."

We got in his car and he glanced at me before powering up the engine. "Close your eyes."

I shot him a look. "You can't ask a girl to close her eyes before driving her somewhere. That's creepy."

Mason sighed. "Come on. Please?"

I smiled, then closed my eyes. As we drove, he turned on my favorite oldies station. We only drove for a couple of minutes before he stopped the car. "We're here."

I opened my eyes and stared at the rec center. "What are we doing here?"

He turned to me. "Don't you remember? This is where we first met. I mean, officially. You were going swimming with your friends, and you ran smack into me in the hall outside the locker room."

My cheeks burned. I remembered that day and that horrible blue one-piece swimsuit I was wearing. "Oh yeah. We were here swimming for Rosalie's birthday. And you, Jude, and Zed spent the rest of the time acting like fools on the high dive."

He looked sheepish. "I was trying to get your attention. To impress you."

I snorted. "By being loud and obnoxious and making as big of a splash as you could?"

"It's what freshman boys do."

"I can't believe you remembered this. I didn't."

"You were the hottest girl I had ever seen."

I scoffed. "Whatever. I was the only girl not wearing a two-piece. And I had the worst hair back then."

"You didn't know how pretty you were, and that's what made you beautiful."

I laughed. "You've been listening to the oldies' station too much. That's a line from one of the songs."

Mason drove us to the movie theater next. "Do you know why I brought you here?"

I was catching on. "This is where we first held hands. Mason, that was only six months ago. Of course I remember."

He nodded, a blush staining his cheeks. "You know that you're the only girl I've ever held hands with?"

"And you're the only boy I've ever held hands with." I grabbed his hand.

He rubbed the back of my hand with his thumb. "I know why I never had. My mom. She never let me hang out in a group with girls in middle school. Then I met you freshman year, and I never wanted to hold anyone else's."

A warm feeling curled in my belly. "I guess I had been waiting for you since freshman year, too."

"I kind of wish we hadn't wasted so much time. Why did it take us this long to get together?"

I reached up and rubbed the back of his neck. "Because we were kids, and it didn't matter then. But now we have all the time in the world, right?"

Mason turned to me. "Ashlyn, I know you don't want to talk about it, but I want to talk about the Air Force Academy again. I really believe this is the best move for our future. It's an actual career I can be proud of. One that means I can provide for a family. I just wasn't excited about becoming a pastor, and don't you think pastors, of all people, should be excited about their job?"

I looked out the window at the movie theater, remembering the thrill of his hand on mine for the first time. "I'm just disappointed that we can't be in school together. I can't go to the Air Force Academy, so I can't be on campus with you."

"But you could go to the Colorado Springs campus of the University of Colorado. You'd be close by. And the Academy campus isn't a closed campus. It's not a jail. I can leave when I have time, and we could still study together."

I thought for a moment. "A state school would be cheaper than Eckman University."

Mason smiled. "Yes it would. But you'd need to apply now. Will you?"

"I mean, I probably will. But Mason, you have to know how hurt I was that you planned all this without me. Are we going to be a team or not? Because you can't keep major life decisions from me like this."

Mason nodded and looked down. "I'm so sorry about that. I told myself I was protecting you in case it didn't work out, but I was really protecting myself."

My heart squeezed for a moment as I remembered all the secrets I had been keeping from him. The Storm Chasers meetings, the trip to Nashville, the tornados. I thought for a moment about telling him, but stopped. I didn't want to fight about them again. Besides, this didn't matter anymore. I was done with the Storm Chasers.

I leaned toward Mason. "I forgive you. I understand, and yes, I'll try to get into UCCS. I mean, I'm already accepted at Eckman, but I can try, right?"

He nodded. "I guess the worst-case scenario is you go to Eckman for one year to get some classes under your belt, and then you could transfer to UCCS after that."

My throat became thick. "I would hate that. I don't want to be away from you for a year."

He brushed some hair out of my eyes. "Hey. It would be okay. As an Air Force wife, we'd have times when we're apart. Months or a year. For deployments. I think sometimes spouses get to go. But sometimes they don't."

I had never heard Mason mention marriage before. I had thought about it a million times, but I didn't know he had. That made me so happy. But the thought of being separated from him for deployments made me sad. Did I really want to be married to someone in the military? Why wasn't I given a choice in this matter?

"Air Force wife, huh?"

He blushed. "Uh, I just meant that if we're in this for the long haul, there could be times where we're not in the same place. But we could deal. I mean, with video chat and bullet trains, we can never be that far apart, right?"

I laughed as he squirmed. "Yeah, I get what you're saying."

We left the movie theater and drove to Cactus Kitchen to get dinner and use my com to figure out the application process to the UCCS. We brainstormed ideas on where we could meet around the Air Force Academy for study sessions.

We had just finished eating when Mason looked at his com. "Oh my gosh. It's seven o'clock. I should be home now. Mom is going to kill me."

We paid at the tablet on the table and hurried out the door. I felt a flash of anger toward Mrs. Woods. Our afternoon had been amazing, and she was ruining it, not just by giving Mason a ridiculous curfew for a senior in high school, but because now he was upset about making her mad. I pushed aside the thought that he was putting her above me. That was ridiculous.

He drove me to the school so I could pick up my car. I turned to him before getting out of his car. "Thank you for the best date ever. I really love you, Mason."

He grabbed my hand and pulled me toward him. "And I really love you."

We leaned toward each other, and met in a long, slow kiss. I didn't want it to end, but I also didn't want him getting into more trouble with his mom. We just needed to play by

her rules for a few more months. I finally broke away, and
he groaned.

He smacked his forehead. "Uh, I meant to talk to you
about prom. I forgot."

"Let's meet at our park table tomorrow, okay? After
school? We can talk about it then."

"Yeah, okay."

I exited the car and leaned back before closing the door.
"Bye, Mason."

"Bye, Ash."

He gave me the best smile before pulling away. I was on
cloud nine. I got in my car and put it on auto-pilot so I could
stay up there a little longer. But I crashed back to earth
when I got home in time to see the stack of boxes next to
Mella's car.

CHAPTER 22

I was staring at the boxes when the front door banged open.

"A little help here?" Mella grunted as she struggled down the steps.

I took a deep breath and tied my heart balloon to my bag, then set the bag on the ground. I walked over and grabbed the top box from the stack in her arms. "Polite people say, 'Would you help me, please?'"

She put her box next to the stack already on the ground. "You're right. I'm sorry." She opened her trunk, then took the box from my arms.

I helped her put the boxes in the trunk and in the backseat of her car without another word. It's what a grown-up would do; help someone even when they didn't want to.

She closed her trunk, then turned to me. "Thanks, Baby Sis. I mean it."

I nodded, then grabbed my bag and balloon and turned to go inside. She threw her arm around my shoulders and walked with me. "Where have you been? And what's with the balloon?"

I couldn't stop the smile from dancing across my lips. "Out with Mason. It's our six-monthaversary. He took me to all our firsts."

She arched an eyebrow. "Your firsts? First what?"

"Where we first met, and first held hands, and first..." I stopped.

"First kiss?" She wiggled her eyebrows and poked me in the side.

I swatted her hand away. "That's none of your business."

She laughed and followed me up the stairs and into my room. "Aw, I'm sorry. I don't mean to embarrass you."

I set my bag on my desk and refused to turn around. "Yes, you do."

My bed creaked as she plunked down. "Fine, you're right. But only because you're my sister. But seriously, I'm happy for you. Mason is a great guy."

I fingered the ribbon on the balloon. "Yeah, he is. Did you hear he's going into the Air Force?"

"What? What about Eckman?"

I flopped on the bed next to her. "Apparently he had been trying to get into the Air Force Academy, and didn't tell me because it's so hard to get in. That's why he let me go on and on about our stupid plans for Eckman."

Mella narrowed her eyes and pursed her lips. "Hmm. Well, that makes sense now."

"What does?"

"Why Mom and Chip were talking about the Air Force Academy last week. I overheard them talking about how Chip helped someone get in by connecting them with a senator. Mom was thanking him for some reason. She must have been thanking him for getting Mason in."

I groaned. "Ugh, don't remind me about Chip's part in this. I was just starting to maybe like him."

"Like who? Chip?"

I rolled over on my back and stared at the ceiling. "I heard him and Mom outside yesterday. The way he was talking to her made me think he actually cares about her. I thought it might be time to give him a chance. But he's directly responsible for Mason changing his plans."

Mella laid down next to me. "So you were going to give Chip a chance?"

"I don't know. I guess so. I mean, I'm just so confused. I really believe Dad is still alive." I sat up and held my hand up. "And don't give me a lecture right now. I get that none of you believe he's alive, so I understand why you are all moving on."

"This sounds intense." Trig poked his head in my room. "I want in."

Mella sat up and patted the bed, and I groaned. "Please don't gang up on me."

Trig wrapped his arm around me. "We're not going to gang up. Right, Mel?"

"Right. We're just listening."

I sighed. "So since I don't have a better option right now, I thought I'd try going with the flow, which meant giving Chip a chance. Besides, now that..." I broke off. I had almost spilled what the Storm Chasers wanted mc to do.

"Now that, what?" Penn jumped into my room and flopped on the bed. The bed gave a horrible creak.

"Penn! You almost broke my bed," I shouted.

Penn looked almost sorry. "Oops."

They all stared at me, waiting for me to finish. I flopped back down and buried my head under my pillow. "Never mind."

"Hmm. Time for an Ash Pile!" Penn yelled before flopping on top of me.

I grunted as the weight of all three of my siblings pressed me down on the bed. "No! Stop, ugh! We're too old for this!" They were all laughing hysterically. And then someone started tickling my side, and I twisted, pinching whatever skin I could find.

"Ouch! Gosh, Ash. When did you learn to pinch so hard?" By the time I could sit up, Trig was rubbing his arm and Penn was giving me a dirty look.

"It took me eighteen years to perfect that," I said, smoothing down my hair and scooting so my back was against the headboard of my bed.

Mella had made her way to my desk chair in the melee. "I'll catch you boys up. Mason is going to the Air Force Academy, and Chip was the one who helped him get in, and Ashlyn just remembered that, so she's bummed that she was about to give Chip a chance. Also, she still thinks Dad is alive."

The boys' eyes glazed over the way they always did when they found themselves in the middle of girl drama. Everyone was quiet for a few minutes. I didn't mind that Mella told them my issues. In fact, I felt better. There's something so cleansing about getting things out in the open.

"I miss onion rings," Penn said. We all stared at him. "Dad was the one who would take me to get onion rings. You know how Mom hates them. I haven't had onion rings since he left."

"I don't want to eat smores anymore," Mella said. "I was at a camp out with my volleyball team two years after Dad left, and they made smores, and I started bawling the minute I took a bite. Because he made the best smores. And now I can't eat them."

Trig snorted. "You all make Dad sound like some foodie. I only mow the lawn every week, because he had taught me the week before he left. I wanted to make him proud when he got back by showing him how good I was at it. The sound of the lawn mower reminds me about him."

No one spoke for a few moments. I thought hearing these things would make me sad, but it didn't. It made me feel closer to my siblings.

Mella finally broke the silence. "Baby Sis, we can talk about Dad whenever you want. It would have helped you if we had talked about him more these past ten years."

A tear dripped down my face. "Thanks. That'll be hard to do with you all gone, but thanks."

Trig reached over and messed up my hair. "We're not dying, kid. We're just living outside this house."

I glared at him and batted his hand away. "Duh. I understand why you're all moving. I just wish you weren't all going at once."

Mella looked wistful. "Yeah, I can see that wasn't the best way to handle this."

"Let's go back to Mason," Trig said. "I didn't know Chip had gotten him into the Air Force Academy."

Mella repeated what she heard for the boy's sake. "And now Ash is changing her mind about giving Chip a chance."

"It's not the only reason."

All three of my siblings leaned forward. "Seriously, Ash. Tell us," Trig said.

I took a deep breath. "Look, don't give me any crap, but I've gone to a couple Storm Chaser meetings. And I've learned some things about the hurricane that make me question everything that Chip is doing as the head of USHA."

Mella opened her mouth, but Trig held out his hand. "What have you learned?"

"There's this area called the Disaster Zone in Alabama. It's a wasteland that has been ravaged by tornadoes that spawn off the hurricane."

Mella shrugged. "Yeah, we all know that hurricanes can cause tornados inland."

"Tornadoes that show up every three months on the dot?"

They all looked at each other. "What do you mean?"

"I've been there. I went to the Disaster Zone on Saturday and while we were there, three tornadoes dropped out of the sky. Luca said the Storm Chasers had been monitoring the area for five years, and the tornadoes show up every three months."

"Who's Luca?"

"You were there?"

"How did you get there?"

All their questions came at once. And they all sounded angry, rather than inquisitive.

I slouched back against my headboard. "Luca is a guy I met at one of the meetings. His dad is one of the leaders of the Storm Chasers. He and I took a bullet train to Nashville on Saturday morning, then took a plane from the Storm Chasers headquarters into the Disaster Zone. He needed footage, and I wanted to see the storm up close."

Mella's face became stone. "I can't believe you did that."

"I need to know, Mella! I needed to see. And I get why they have the theories that they do."

Trig rubbed the back of his neck. "And you think this has something to do with Chip?"

I threw my hands up. "I don't know. There's a shady vibe from the hurricane. The clouds looked like they were pressed against a wall, or a barrier that was keeping them in place. And the line for the Disaster Zone? It's perfectly straight. And tornadoes showing up every three months? Of course, people stay away from that area! How has nobody noticed the pattern?"

"Because the news doesn't talk about it," Penn said.

I clapped my hands together. "Exactly. And why doesn't the news talk about it?"

Mella shook her head. "Come on, Ash. This road leads nowhere and will only leave you feeling foolish."

I glared at her. "Thanks. Anyway, don't worry. I'm done with the Storm Chasers."

"Why?"

I couldn't bring myself to tell them what they had asked me to do with Mom's access card. As much as I didn't want to be a part of them, I also didn't want to give Mella any more reason to hate on them.

"Their meetings are just a bunch of fundraisers to get money for their team to go protest in Washington." That was a safe enough reason. "It doesn't matter, anyway. I'm ready to focus on what's next. What's next for you all is getting your crap out of the house. What's next for me is prom."

Penn batted his eyes at me. "Ooo, prom. What color dress should I wear?" I threw a pillow at him, and he dodged it, laughing. We spent the next hour talking about my sibling's experiences at prom. It was a great way to end the night. I really loved my life. There was no reason to spoil it by chasing hurricanes. It was time to move on.

CHAPTER 23

"WHERE'S YOUR BARNACLE?" ROSALIE wiggled her eyebrows at me as she plopped her lunch bag on our table.

I looked around and shrugged as I unscrewed the cap to my bottled water.

Dasha slid onto the seat next to me. "Mason hasn't been eating with us this week. Are you okay?"

"Yeah, trouble in paradise?" Rosalie laughed, then stopped as soon as she caught Dasha's death glare.

"No, we're fine. I mean, we had a small fight, but we got it all worked out."

"Didn't you see the balloon on her locker yesterday?" Gretchen shoved Rosalie.

Rosalie threw her hands in the air. "Oh yeah! I saw that. So. Cute."

I tried to suppress a grin. "It was our six-monthaversary. Mason took me on a tour of our firsts."

Rosalie leaned forward. "Ooo, first what?"

"You know, the first time we met, the first time he told me he liked me, the first time we held hands-"

"The first time you 'you know," Gretchen said, a wicked smile on her face.

I threw a napkin at her. "If you mean kiss, then yes. That's all the 'you know' we're going to do until marriage."

Rosalie sighed and chomped into her banana. "Okay, fine."

None of the boys showed up for lunch, which was fine with me. It took the spotlight off the fact that Mason wasn't eating with us. I was a little concerned about that, but I tried not to worry. Besides, we were meeting at the park later.

It didn't occur to me until my last class that he might be planning a promposal. Trig and Mella nearly died laughing last night, reminiscing about an old tradition where guys asked girls to prom in elaborate ways with props and signs. No one at our school did anything like that, but Mason was an old soul. Our table in the park would be perfect for something like that. Maybe the balloon on my locker yesterday was just the beginning.

My heart dropped a little when I got to the park and saw him just sitting there. I took a deep breath and laughed at myself for getting so worked up. He gave me a soft grin as I trotted up to him. A bitter breeze pressed in, reminding us that snow could still wallop us in March, so I hopped up next to him and snuggled in as close as I could.

"Yikes, this was a bad idea. It's too cold. Should we go somewhere else?"

He put his arm around me and rubbed my shoulder. "No, let's stay. The fresh air feels nice."

I shoved my hands in my pockets. "Have you ever heard of a promposal?"

"A what?"

"A promposal. Where a guy asks a girl to prom using signs and puns and props."

Mason looked at me like I was crazy. "No."

I pressed my lips together, my cheeks heating. "Oh. It's something Trig and Mella were talking about last night. Anyway, let's talk prom."

He pulled me a little tighter and scuffed his shoe on the stone bench. "What do you want to do?"

I was getting a weird vibe from him. I never liked it when he got into a non-committal mood and put everything on me. What if I asked for something that was too much? "I guess just the standard stuff. I'll get a dress, you wear a tux. Or just a suit is fine."

"Uh, I guess I'll have to get something."

"Which will be fine, right? A suit is always a good thing to have. Don't do a tux. That's way over the top."

Mason rubbed the back of his neck. "They'll give me a dress uniform in the Air Force Academy."

I swallowed. "Oh. Well, we can figure out what you wear later. It's not that big a deal. How about we all rent a limo and go together as a group?"

"How much are those?"

I shrugged. "I don't know. Kids do it for prom all the time, so it can't be too bad, right? And I'll chip in too; you don't have to pay for everything for me."

He nodded and pulled his arm off my shoulder. He stared at his hands, not saying anything.

I didn't want to be one of those girls who was worried about every feeling her boyfriend had. But Mason hadn't looked at me since I got there.

"You okay?"

He nodded and rubbed his hands on his legs. "What else?"

"Well, there's dinner before prom. We can take the limo to dinner, then it can take us to prom. Prom is at the

Broncos stadium, so we could find a restaurant between here and there. Somewhere in Castle Pines, or Lone Tree? Ooo, how about sushi?"

Mason got off the table and began to pace. "Ashlyn, I can't do this."

I watched him, my stomach sinking. "We don't have to do sushi."

"No, I can't do prom like this."

I bit my lip and tried to stay calm. "What do you mean? Is it the money?"

He shook his head and kept walking back and forth in front of me. I waited for him to say something, the cold of the table seeping into my jeans.

After a few minutes, he stopped, took a deep breath, and stared at the ground. "I've been doing a lot of thinking. My mom is right. It would be more fair to both of us if we spent the next few years free."

"Free?"

"Yeah, free. Free to not worry about anything and focus on the next steps of our lives. We're so young and have so much to figure out. Don't you want to be free?"

My heart pounded. I didn't want to say out loud what I thought he might be trying to tell me. "Free from what?"

"Well, free from each other. I guess I just don't want to have to think about you while I'm in training at the Academy and trying to learn how to live on my own, away from my parents."

My mouth dropped and for a second I couldn't breathe. "Excuse me?"

Mason finally looked at me in the eyes, his look pleading. He grabbed my hands. "And you shouldn't have to think about me, either. Trust me, it'll be better this way."

I yanked my hands back. "Better if you don't have to think about me."

He shrugged. "I mean, yeah. We can still go to the prom together. But I just felt like I should tell you this so you don't go with any wrong ideas."

I jumped up, rage pounding in my head. "Let me recap. You want to go to prom, but only if I understand that we're not together, because you don't want to have to think about me anymore. Because that's what your mommy told you to do."

Mason gave me a look of pity. Pity. "Come on, Ash. If this is real, it'll survive some time apart, right? You'll do so much better if you can just focus on yourself."

I scoffed. "Don't pretend like you're doing this for me. But thanks for proving that your mom calls all the shots in your life. Is she going with you to the Air Force Academy, too? You gonna bunk with her?"

Mason's face clouded over. "It's not about her."

I waved my hand. "Whatever. Got it, loud and clear. Bye Mason."

I stormed off and jumped in my car, peeling out of the parking lot fast enough that the safety alarms started sounding. I put the car on autopilot to head back to school. I wasn't ready to go home yet, and didn't know where else to go.

As soon as I was in the school parking lot, I pulled out my com and blocked Mason from our family tracking app. He no longer had the right to see where I was. Then I sat back in disbelief. What had just happened? How could he plan that amazing date yesterday, and then today turn around and tell me that he didn't want to have to think about me anymore?

I don't know how long I had been sitting there when my com buzzed. I almost didn't check it. I didn't want to talk to anyone. The humiliation of being rejected by Mason was still so raw that I couldn't imagine having a normal conversation with anyone. But years of conditioning to answer all texts won out. I checked my com, then groaned. It was Luca.

> **Hey. I am sorry about Sunday. Can we meet?**

I thought for a few seconds. I needed to go somewhere, even if it meant seeing him.

> **Sure. Right now?**

> **Yes. How about the coffee shop in Castle Pines?**

> **Perfect. Be there in fifteen.**

I entered the coffee shop's address into my autopilot and let the car handle it. My thoughts jumped all over the place on the ride there. Mason just dumped me. The Storm Chasers wanted my mom's access card. And Luca was telling me he was sorry. Did that mean he didn't want my mom's card anymore?

I arrived at the coffee shop sooner than I thought. My scattered brain settled on relief at how close Castle Pines was to Castle Rock. Trig and Penn wouldn't be so far after all. I shook away those thoughts and entered the coffee shop, immediately spotting Luca at a table with another guy.

I froze as Luca stood up, with the other guy close behind. It was Silas Chapman. I narrowed my eyes and cautiously approached the table.

"This is sorry?" I demanded. "This is an ambush."

Luca had the sense to seem ashamed. "It's not an ambush. I really am sorry. And you should listen to Silas."

Silas held up his hands in surrender. "It was my idea. Don't get mad at him."

"What was your idea? The ambush? Asking me to betray my mom?" I folded my arms.

He sighed. "I should have reached out to you sooner and not let Luca take the lead. I'm sorry about that. But you know that my brother and your dad were friends, right?"

It all came back to me. Silas' brother was Mateo, my dad's partner at USHA. The one who stayed behind when Dad went into the storm.

"Please, sit," Silas said. Curiosity got the better of me and I sat down, clutching my bag to my chest like it was going to protect me.

Luca slipped over to the counter while Silas spoke.

"My brother is our contact inside the storm. He's hunkered down at a shelter fifty miles in. Shelters are spaced ten miles apart, while our communication range is currently limited to fifty miles. He and a team have been in the storm for five years, looking for a way to get further.

The only thing stopping them right now is the problem with communications."

I narrowed my eyes. "How do they get supplies? How do they get between the shelters?"

Silas chuckled and sat back. "All good questions. Let me start at the beginning. Your dad and my brother were the first to discover that the storm wasn't natural. Mateo still won't tell me what they found, but apparently there is data within USHA. As soon as they found it out, they knew that the only way to expose the secret was to get inside the storm and gather irrefutable evidence."

Luca returned and set down a chocolate croissant in front of me. I glared at him. "I don't want your dirty food offering."

He sighed and looked at Silas. "Did you get to the good part yet?"

Silas shook his head. "I'm getting there. The only record Mateo will tell me about is the shelter network. There are a series of shelters every ten miles into the storm. It's too coincidental to deny someone intentionally built them to navigate the storm."

"But that would have to mean that they knew the storm was going to stay. How could they have known that?" I tried to ignore the croissant, but smelling warm bread and chocolate made me salivate. I picked it up, took a bite, and scowled at Luca's triumphant look.

"The only logical conclusion is they had the technology to make the storm. We just don't know why or what that technology is yet. We have to get to the eye to find the answers."

I took another bite of my croissant. "And so your brother and my dad were going to go investigate this ten years ago. Only, your brother didn't because of a sinus infection."

Silas nodded. "All I can tell you is that it almost destroyed Mateo. He was a wreck for about a year after your dad disappeared. I finally learned enough from him when he was ready to talk about it that I called up Tyler and we formed the Storm Chasers."

Luca went back to the counter and returned with a cup of water for me. "Dad and Silas have been building the Storm Chasers ever since. With the storm about to weaken, we have to try to make it to the Eye."

Silas leaned forward. "Mateo says the best way to get through is to set up a communications relay. They need supplies in order to do that. We need to assign someone every fifty miles so they can relay communications back to safety. If we set up our own network, then we'll be able to get in to get the answers we need."

I wiped my hands on the napkin, crumbled it, and handed Luca the trash. "And you need my mom's access card to do it."

Silas nodded. "I'm not going to lie. We've been trying to figure out how to get the tech we need for a long time, and then suddenly here you are. Right when the storm is about to weaken at the exact time we need it to. I'd say this is serendipitous, don't you?"

All the pieces did seem to be lining up.

"Si," Luca said. "Show her the good part."

Silas studied my face for a second. "I'm not trying to be pushy or anything, but I have one more thing to show you that I hope convinces you." He stopped, pulled out his com and scrolled through an app. He found what he was looking for and turned the com to me. "Look at this."

The picture displayed a log of some sort. Silas had zoomed in on my dad's name, and the date. I gasped. "Is that date right? Three years ago?"

Silas nodded. "Everyone signs into the shelters each time they go in. Mateo found your dad's name on the one fifty miles in. Which means he's been to that one in the last three years. Or, at least we think so."

My heart pounded. I couldn't believe I was considering this. Unbidden, Mason's words echoed in my mind.

I don't want to have to think about you anymore.

It wasn't just him. My siblings were moving on. Mom was moving forward with Chip. Despite what everyone said, there was evidence proving Dad did not die ten years ago. It was three years old, but it was evidence.

Everyone was forging their own paths and burning bridges to do it. Maybe it was time for me to do the same.

I looked Luca in the eye. "I'll get you the card."

CHAPTER 24

I WASN'T GOING TO tell anyone about me and Mason. It was too humiliating. I almost wished he had cheated on me or something. I could have blubbered all day to my family and friends about that, and they would have been on my side. Rosalie and Gretchen would have organized a revenge prank, like egging the Woods' house. And I would have bought them the eggs.

But I just couldn't bring myself to tell anyone that he didn't want to have to think about me anymore. That I was a weight, holding him back. A ball and chain. A wet blanket.

I made it through the whole next day and almost all of Friday with my secret. My friends didn't question why Mason wasn't eating with us again. I was glad he had already set that precedence. But Mom was waiting for me when I got home Friday afternoon. She called me into the family room as soon as I got in the house.

"Honey." She patted the seat next to her on the couch.

I dropped my bag on the armchair and sat, eyeing her warily. "Mom."

She put her arm around me and pulled me close. "Why didn't you say anything?"

"About..."

She sighed. "Mason called me. He said that you guys decided to spend the next few years apart."

I snorted as my throat closed. "We decided? That's what he told you? He's lying. His mom decided." I couldn't believe he called my mom. Man, he got to call all the shots, didn't he?

Mom searched my eyes. "So it wasn't your choice?"

"No, it wasn't my choice. Nothing is my choice, is it? He got to choose how to spend his future, without even including me in it. And so do the rest of you."

She laid her head on mine. "You get to choose too."

I pushed myself away and sat back, glaring at her. "But not really. If I could choose, Mason and I would go to Eckman like we had planned last year. And my family would still be here. Including Dad."

She twisted her mouth, but didn't start a lecture. That surprised me. I looked down at my hands and tried to calm my thoughts.

She spoke after a few minutes of silence. "You'll get through this. I'm sorry everything looks different from what you planned, but sometimes amazing things can grow when they have the space to do so. And so often, unexpected change creates space that we didn't even know we needed."

That gave me an idea. I swallowed and nodded. "I guess you're right. I mean, I hate it, but there's nothing I can do about it now, right?" I leaned back into Mom. She took the bait and pulled me close again.

"What do you want to do now? I mean, like right now. Let's take one day at a time. Want to go out for dinner? Watch movies all night? Mella will be home soon. We can have a girls' night. I told Chip that I needed to be home tonight, so I don't have any plans."

"I was going to sleep over at Dasha's house."

Mom stuck out her lower lip. "Are you sure? You don't want to hang out with me?"

I reached out and patted her cheek. "I love you, but this is the kind of thing I need my best friend for." My stomach twisted. I hated lying to her, especially when she looked so eager to help me through my heartbreak. But for the first time, I was glad that Mason was such a jerk. It gave me the excuse I needed to be out of the house tonight. "What about tomorrow? I'll be home by noon. How about lunch, then pedicures?"

She pulled me in and kissed my forehead. "I love that plan."

I threw my arms around her and held her while I tried to come up with a plan to get her access card without her knowing about it. I had to think fast. "Are there any aloe face masks left? I thought Dasha and I could do skin treatments tonight."

She gave me a last squeeze and stood up. "Yes. They're in my bathroom in the top drawer. No, wait. I think I left them in the bathtub. Oh, just hold on. I'll go get them for you."

She left the room, and I made myself stay seated until I heard the final creak at the top of the stairs. I hurried into the kitchen and found her purse sitting on the counter. She kept her card and her ID badge on a lanyard that was hanging out of the purse. I quickly unclipped the access card, leaving her badge and her lanyard. If the lanyard was visible from her purse, hopefully she wouldn't think to check it.

I shoved the card in my back pocket and tore up the stairs just as Mom was coming out of her room.

"Here you go. Are you sure you don't want to stay home with your momma tonight?"

I took the packages, then gave her another hug. "I'm sure. I love you, Mom. Thanks for everything."

Mom hugged me back. "Be safe tonight."

Guilt churned in my stomach. "I will. I promise."

I almost forgot to put some clothes in a bag, like I was really going to Dasha's. Then I smacked my head. I had one more loose end to tie up before I could meet up with the Storm Chasers.

I checked my com, then drove straight to Dasha's house. This time I was glad for her community college course day. It meant she was home.

I rang the doorbell, and Mr. Hart answered.

"Ashlyn! My favorite Booker. I didn't know you were coming. Neither did Tamika. She would have planned something way better than instant food pods. You know that we only get true home-cooked meals when you come over." He wrapped me in a hug.

I smiled. "I'm not staying or anything. I just need to see Dasha."

Mr. Hart pouted. "Okay, fine. She's in her cave."

I ran down the stairs and burst into Dasha's room. She shrieked and threw a pillow at the door. "Julian!"

I ducked. "No, it's me!"

She clutched her chest and fell onto her bed. "Ash! I thought you were my dumb brother, barging in without knocking."

I closed the door behind me. "I don't blame you. That was an excellent reaction time. And good aim."

She laughed. "What are you doing here? Did I miss something? Were we supposed to go somewhere?"

I tried to slow my breathing. "No, and I can't stay right now. I just need two favors. First, can I come back and spend the night? But not until way later. Like, after midnight."

Dasha leaned forward, her eyes sparkling. "Of course. Ooo, this sounds good. You and Mason going somewhere?"

I shook my head and scowled. "No, we broke up. I mean, Mrs. Woods told Mason to break up with me, and he obeyed his mommy like a good little boy."

Dasha's mouth dropped open. "What? Are you joking?"

"No, but I don't have time for that. I can tell you when I get back. The second thing is, I need to switch coms with you."

"Okay, what's going on?"

I spilled the story about the USHA raid. When I finished, Dasha gave me a blank stare. "Are you kidding me?"

"No. And I really need to go. Mom needs to see my phone here because I told her I was staying the night. But I'm not dumb enough to do this without a com. And that way you can track me."

"Girl, this is the only sensible thing you've said. I can't believe you've gotten yourself in with this crazy group."

"Did you hear what I said about my dad?"

"How can you be sure it was real?"

My heart sank. Why did it always come back to this? Why was I the only one who trusted in a clue that might lead to Dad?

"You're right, Dash. I mean, maybe you're right. But it is something I have to check out. I can't live knowing that there is maybe some evidence out there that will prove to everyone what I know to be true in my heart, but do nothing about it." I checked the time on my com. "I have to go, but there's more I want to tell you. Can I take your com? And can I come back here to stay?"

Dasha sighed and handed me her com. "Yeah, okay. But I'm tracking you the entire night. And come around to the basement door whenever you get back. Mom and Dad don't need to know about this."

I grabbed her in a hug. "You're my best friend in the whole world. I promise I'll tell you everything."

Dasha wouldn't let me break the hug. "Do you promise you aren't doing this because you're sad about Mason? That it's not some self-destructive thing?"

I leaned back and looked her in the eye. "I promise it's not that. For real."

"Be careful, Ashlyn. This sounds nuts."

"I will. It'll be quick, in and out." I blew her a kiss, then ran back up the stairs.

"You really can't stay?" Mr. Hart called out as I sailed toward the door.

"No, I'm so sorry. Rain check?"

"Sure, Baby Girl. Hey, I'm proud of you."

I stopped and looked at him, putting Dasha's com behind my back. He sat on the couch with his tablet, looking like I imagined my dad would look. "You are?"

"Absolutely. I don't have much time left with you or Dasha before you head off into the world to make your mark, so I just want to tell you every time I see you."

Those words made my throat close up. "Thanks, Mr. Hart."

"Wyatt."

"Mr. Hart." I grinned at him, then hurried out the door.

I met Luca at the back of the parking lot next to the light rail station.

We took his car to an old strip mall a few miles away. He led the way into a sketchy-looking Asian restaurant. The Storm Chasers team took up the only tables in the room.

I raised an eyebrow at Luca.

"The owner has been with the Storm Chasers for years. Most of his business is catering and takeout, but he lets us use the dining room for mission planning."

I shrugged and sat down at the end of the table next to Luca. The entire group from the storage unit on Sunday was already there. Ginger and Sybil smiled, and Silas grinned and gave me a chin up nod. Jack and Miri were at our end of the table, chowing down on potstickers.

"Did you get it?" Tyler growled at me.

I glared at him. "Of course I did. Would I be here if I didn't?"

Silas cleared his throat. "So, are we all set?"

Luca leaned forward. "Go over the plan again. Ashlyn wasn't there when we finalized it."

"Because she was outside crying about her mommy," Tyler muttered.

I rolled my eyes. "Forgive me, High Master Denzio, for taking a moment to come to terms with the gravity of betraying my mom's trust for the sake of your cause."

Willie burst out laughing. "This girl's got spunk. I love it."

"I'm here now, and I'm in," I said. "And I hope you planned for me to be on the team that gets inside."

Tyler shook his head. "No way. No kids on the inside team."

I folded my arms across my chest. "No one goes in unless I do. I handle the access card. I am not handing it over to any of you. Besides, I know the layout. And I even know the security guards. If we run into any of them, I can just tell them that my mom sent me to her office to pick up something she forgot."

"She's right," Ginger said. "It'll go faster if we have someone who is familiar with the inside."

Tyler sighed. "Okay, fine. Ashlyn, Willie, Ginger, Sybil, Silas, and myself will go in the side door. Luca, Miri, and Jack will be outside. Jack will monitor the police scanner for any calls related to the building. Luca and Miri, you patrol the perimeter and tell us if you see anyone coming."

Jack, Miri, and Luca all nodded. "You got this," Miri whispered to me.

"Ashlyn, you lead the way. The rest of us will stay behind you. You can signal when it's safe to move forward. Once we get to the office, Ashlyn, you watch the door while we try to find what we need."

I had a thought. "Hold on. I can get you in the building, but I'm not sure my mom's card can access every office."

Silas leaned back in his chair. "Oh, don't worry about that. We have ways of neutralizing doors. We just didn't want to do that to an exterior door, because that would set off an alarm. The office doors are locked, but they are not monitored by alarms."

My heart pounded. "I only have an access card. I don't have the codes to any alarms."

Hugh shook his head. "The access cards disarm the exterior alarms."

"How do you know this?"

"Because they used my company for security." He grinned. "Best account I've ever gotten."

I let out a nervous laugh. "Oh. Okay, do you know whose office we need to get into?"

"What we need is in a special file room," Tyler said. "The one that's located in Chip Sinclair's office."

CHAPTER 25

THE STORM CHASERS HAD argued for a long time at the restaurant about what time to go in. I wanted to get it over with, but Tyler insisted on waiting until eleven o'clock.

I hated to admit that he was right. We arrived at the building at nine o'clock and parked just beyond the perimeter of the property in the dark. There were still so many lights on in the offices. USHA employees, working late on a Friday night, appeared to have no personal life. So we waited. And now there was no one left in the building. Well, no one working anyway. I knew there were security guards.

We made it into the building with no problems. It was frighteningly easy. We simply walked up to a door at the back, and the door clicked open when I held up the card to a panel on the side. The door led to a stairwell that echoed the tiniest sound. We inched up the stairs to the eighth floor. It had taken way too long, but any faster, and the metal stairs sang out our presence.

I took a deep breath. The USHA building was so creepy at night, and my breathing sounded like an enormous snorting gorilla. I tried to open the door that led to the floor without making any sound, but the click of the handle cracked off like a gunshot.

I almost screamed when a hand clasped my shoulder.

"Shhh." Tyler held his finger to his lips and was speaking just above a whisper. "Can you see anyone?"

I glared at him, then peeked out into the hall. It was dark, except for the occasional security light on the ceiling every twenty feet. Chills rant down my arms. This was a terrible idea. Once we got in the hall, our only option was to move forward. If a guard on patrol came around and saw us, we'd be toast.

It was now or never. I swallowed hard, then motioned for everyone to stay. Tyler pulled me in and spoke close to my ear, his breath hot on my cheek. "Luca just spotted two cars entering the parking lot. We have to hurry."

As if I needed the extra pressure. I nodded, then hurried down the hall and peeked around the corner. It was clear. I waved the group in, and they slipped in behind me. Their stealthy, coordinated movements shocked me. I wondered if they had done this before, but shook the thought away. No time for that now.

We continued down three more hallways. It only took a few minutes before we were standing outside Chip's office door.

Willie pulled something out of his pocket and handed it to Silas. Ginger and Sybil took up positions with their backs to Silas while he worked at the door handle, blocking any view of what he was doing. Tyler put his finger in his ear and spoke in a low voice over the coms, communicating with the outside team.

I jumped at the sound of a loud pop. I whirled around as Silas pushed into the room. A char mark was on the wall next to the door, and the handle was dangling, making it evident that it was broken.

"What did you do?" I hissed. Tyler grabbed my arm and pulled me into Chip's office with the rest of them.

"Hush. I told you we could neutralize doors."

Panic clawed at my throat. "You didn't say that it would be so obvious!"

Ginger put her arm around my shoulders. "We don't care. We'll be long gone before they find out. Don't worry; they won't be able to trace us."

"Not us. Just my mom." I frowned. I had not thought this through. I looked around the dark office, which was lit well enough by the lights outside the building. One entire wall was floor to ceiling windows, and everything in the office looked expensive. There was an overpowering smell of Chip's cologne, and I almost gagged.

Another loud pop shot out, and Silas pushed open a door behind Chip's desk. "Let's go, people."

I sighed and followed them into a small room. Sybil and Tyler were already pulling at drawers, not caring about the mess they made.

Ginger held up her hands. "Hey. Don't make a mess. They're going to know someone was in here, but let's make it hard for them to figure out what we took."

Tyler grinned. "Now that's a good idea."

I followed Ginger's lead and started cleaning up behind Tyler and Sybil so they could look quickly.

Willie let out a soft shout. "I found the tablets." The other adults crowded around the box he had pulled down, and I kept putting the files that they had scattered back in the drawers.

"This is so weird," I said. "Why is there so much paper in here? Don't they save their files on the cloud?"

Sybil glanced over her shoulder. "The cloud can be hacked. Even the government cloud. For information security, they have backup file rooms like this."

Tyler nodded. "The only way to keep something secret is on paper that only one person has access to."

It shouldn't have surprised me. I knew Chip was devious.

I stared at the thick file in my hand. I wondered if I should take it with me. Mom would never believe me about this file room if I didn't have something to show her. I opened the folder, then froze when I read the paper inside.

I Expenses

My heart beat fast. It was a list of survival supplies, including food rations, cases of water, tarps, radios, batteries, and weather-proofing. Chip's signature was on the bottom of the page. I shuffled through the pages. At the top were dates, going back three months at a time, and Chip's signature was on them all.

I flipped to the back of the file and froze. The very last page had the date that my dad disappeared at the top. I stared at the next line:

Jonah Booker - Lead Delivery

My hands shook as I stared at his name, then Chip's signature at the bottom. The supply list resembled the others, except for some crossed-off items. I flipped back and forth between this page and the others to compare.

The noticeable difference was the line about radios. Someone had changed Dad's list to include only two radios and one extra battery. And someone crossed off the weather-proofing from his list too.

Silas grunted behind me, and I turned to see that he was reading over my shoulder. "Mateo was right. He suspected an issue with Jonah's supplies for the storm. But he could never prove it. Jonah didn't check the packs, because he didn't think he had time. Even though Mateo tried to get him to."

This was it. Finally, my search is over. This piece of evidence connected Chip to my dad's disappearance.

Silas stopped me as I turned to storm out with the file in hand.

"Hold on. You have to put that back."

"No! I need it. I have to show Mom. It's the proof I've been looking for."

He tightened his grip. "Did you see the date on the top page? That's in three weeks. Which means whatever this is, they're going to make a delivery in three weeks. Someone, probably Chip, will be looking for this file."

I shrugged him off. "So what? He'll already know someone was in here. Who cares if he finds out what was taken?"

Sybil came over, her blue eyes soft. "Because if they know that someone took this file, then they might be on the lookout for someone trying to enter the storm. We don't need that kind of attention."

"But won't they know when they figure out that you took the tablets?"

Willie shook his head. "Nah. These tablets have many uses. They won't be able to figure out what app we wanted them for unless they see that file missing."

A tear dripped down my face as I clutched it tighter. I had what I needed. Could I really give it up?

Tyler handed me his ear com. "Here. You need to talk to Luca."

I eyed him, then put it in my ear.

"Ashlyn? Ashlyn, are you there?"

"I'm here."

"You guys gotta go. Jack just heard on the scanner that the police are coming to your area. They should be there in less than five minutes."

"I found a file, Luca. One that proves that Chip sabotaged my dad's mission."

"Are you sure?"

I looked at the file again. "Well, it proves that someone altered his supplies on the day of his mission. Chip's signature is there."

"But that could have been for a lot of reasons. You already knew that Chip was in charge back then."

"But Mom needs to see this! She's dating the guy, Luca. The same guy who did something to get rid of my dad."

The adults were in a small group at the door, having an intense discussion in whispers. Ginger and Willie shoved the tablets in their bags, and everyone looked over at me.

Silas came over. "Ashlyn, we've got to go. And we need you to lead the way again."

"Ashlyn." Luca's voice filled my ear. "Put the file back and come out. We'll find your dad, but not if you're all in jail."

I closed my eyes and handed Silas the file. He placed it on a table, opened it, grabbed his com, and snapped photos of the first and last pages.

"There," he said. "We can study it later."

"Let's go," Tyler hissed.

I rushed out before the others, stopping suddenly when I saw Chip's desk. He had left his digital picture frame on, and it flipped through various images. Most of them were of Chip with dumb things, like a fish he caught or one of his expensive cars. But then an image of my mom popped up. Only it wasn't a picture I had ever seen of her. The picture showed her in a tight crop-top, with her breasts practically spilling out. She was leaning forward, as if she was trying to make them spill out.

But something looked off. I leaned in close and saw the problem. "Oh gross."

"What?" Luca said in my ear.

"Chip photoshopped my mom's face on some half-naked woman. It's one of the images he has on the digital picture frame on his desk."

"Are you serious? Uh, Ashlyn, you guys gotta go. A police car just showed up."

I pulled out Dasha's com and snapped a pic of the abomination before leading the way out of the office.

We went back the way we came, without seeing any security guards. Tyler poked his head out the exterior door to check if the path was clear.

"One at a time, two minutes apart," he whispered. "Ashlyn, you first. Straight for the trees. Walk, don't run. Running always draws unwanted attention."

I nodded, took a deep breath, and headed outside. It was freezing out. But none of us had wanted to risk bulky coats. I looked straight ahead, afraid of what I might see if I looked around. I didn't realize I had been holding my breath until I reached the darkness of the trees and was standing next to Miri.

"Good work, Booker," she said.

I watched the remaining crew members coming out, starting with Ginger, then Willie, Silas, and finally Tyler.

Tyler had barely entered the trees when Sybil peeked out from the door.

"Freeze!" Out of nowhere, two cops rushed toward her, their guns extended. Our group dropped to the ground in the dark behind the bushes.

"What do we do?" I whispered.

"Shhh," Silas said. "Crawl that way. Sybil will be fine; in fact, she'll keep them occupied."

Miri grabbed my arm. "Come on. We have to go. Now."

I had to make myself crawl on my belly after Miri. I was sure that any second a police officer was going to be standing over me, but I kept going. We didn't stop crawling until we reached the van. Jack had the van running, and we all got in. Jack scooted over to let Silas take the driver's seat.

"I think I'm going to throw up," I said.

Luca reached over and squeezed my shoulder. "You did great. We got what we needed. And seriously, don't worry about Sybil."

Tyler grunted. "She was always supposed to go last, in case one of us got caught. Don't worry, she knows what to do."

"Are we gonna leave her?" My voice was squeaky, and I tried to calm myself down.

Miri nodded. "It was part of the contingency plan. She'll get taken to the police station anyway, and she'll call her husband for bail. Don't worry; the Storm Chasers have bail money. She could face charges for breaking and entering, but it's more likely that she'll be released."

My mouth dropped open. "How?"

Willie grinned. "She got a job at USHA last week in housekeeping. Her access card couldn't get us in at all hours, but she'll tell them she fell asleep in the breakroom."

Panic squeezed my belly. "My mom's card! They're going to trace it back to her."

"Give it to me," Tyler ordered. I was too panicked to think straight, so I handed it to him. He wiped the card with a cloth and tossed it out the window of the moving van.

I gasped. "What did you do?"

Tyler turned and looked at me, his eyes full of compassion that I had never seen. "I'm sorry, Ashlyn, but this was always the plan. Trust me, it's better this way."

I started punching his arm. "How could you? She'll never trust me again!"

Luca grabbed my arm. "Think! She'll never know you took it. They'll tell her that her card was used to access the building late at night, and she'll tell them she was home all night, which she was. And when she discovers that it's missing, they'll assume someone somehow stole it. It'll be a dead end."

"And they'll deactivate the card," Miri said.

I tried to calm down as the van headed back to the train station. That was the best-case scenario. I hoped it would work out like that.

Tyler looked at me again. "We couldn't have done all this without you, Ashlyn. Thank you."

I was numb. I just nodded.

CHAPTER 26

Convincing Dasha not to call cops when I texted her about not being there that night took forever. She was sure that I had been kidnapped. But I couldn't leave the group. Not when Ginger and Willie became so excited after hacking into the tablets they had stolen. There was all the data they needed. The trip into the storm was really going to happen.

At five-thirty, I made myself leave the group. Luca walked me to my car. "You sure you don't want to come?"

I shook my head, my heart squeezing. "I can't see how. That's the same week as our senior trip to Seattle. But I'll keep in contact with Miri the whole time. She can keep me posted on how it's going."

"You sound like you're trying to convince me."

"I'm still trying to convince myself. But you don't know how long the mission will last. And I've got to finish school." I wiped a tear off my cheek. "Trust me, no one wants to find my dad more than I do. But the timing isn't right for me. And I trust you."

Luca grabbed my hand. I almost pulled away, then remembered that Mason and I were broken up. His hand was warm and reassuring, so I gripped it tighter.

"I'll find him for you, Ash," he said. My heart melted. It was the first time he had called me Ash.

I nodded. "I gotta go. I'll text you later."

He squeezed my hand before letting it go. I drove as fast as the safety feature would let me back to Dasha's house.

She must have been sitting just inside the walkout basement door. She flung it open as soon as I rounded the corner of the back of her house, and the look she gave me was terrifying. She pulled me inside and closed the door. It was impressive. She made her anger known by closing the door soundlessly, which I had never seen before.

I cautiously handed her com back to her, and she practically threw mine at me. "I can't believe you did that," she hissed, trying to keep her voice in a whisper.

"But we got what we needed, and the Storm Chasers have a real chance of finding Dad."

She sighed. "Can you go back to your own life?"

I shook my head. "No. Not as long as Mom is dating Chip. Oh my gosh." I had almost forgotten. I snatched back Dasha's com and pulled up the pic I had taken of the picture on his desk. "Look."

"Oh, gross."

I nodded, rage curling in my belly again. In the excitement of planning the actual mission into the storm, I had forgotten all about Chip's disgusting behavior. "I'm showing this to Mom." I texted the pic to my phone, then gave her back her com.

We both froze as we heard a sound upstairs. "That's dad. I told you he gets up early. Even on a Saturday."

I reached for the door handle. "I've got to go. I told him I wasn't staying last night, and I don't want him to ask questions."

Dasha wrapped her arms around herself. "I'm going back to bed. I didn't sleep at all, worrying about you."

I grabbed her in a hug. "Thanks, Dash. You're my best friend. Now we can focus on Seattle."

She pushed back and gave a soft squeal. "Yes! Seattle."

I opened the door and waved, then quietly moved around the house, staying out of sight. I moved away from the house and down the block, staying hidden from the Harts' yard. It was pretty amazing how quickly I had learned the art of sneaking around.

I checked my com before I drove away and noticed I had a text from Dasha. I almost laughed out loud when I realized I had sent it myself.

The picture of my mom. Ugh, it was so offensive that I didn't even want Mom to see it.

I almost crashed into the lilac bush in front of our house when I got home. Chip was coming down the steps toward his car. It wasn't even seven o'clock.

I jumped out of the car. "What are you doing here? Were you here all night?" The thought made me want to vomit.

Chip chuckled. "Come on, Ash. You know your mom better than that. Of course not. I was dropping off some donuts."

I hated that he called me 'Ash.' "Don't you have something better to do on a Saturday morning? Why don't you get your own life?"

His eyes turned icy. "When are you going to get it through your head? This is my life. And yours. The sooner you stop fighting it, the sooner we can all get on with the happily ever after part."

Something inside me snapped. "I know you sent my dad into the storm with insufficient supplies." I almost clapped my hand over my mouth, but clenched my fists at my side. I didn't mean to blurt it out, but there it was.

He looked surprised for a brief second, then took a few steps toward me. He lowered his voice. "And what makes you say that?"

I tried to think fast. "The Storm Chasers know a lot more than you give them credit for. They showed me a list of supplies from Dad's mission. A bunch of things were crossed off. Your signature was on it."

His mouth twisted in a smile that didn't reach his eyes. "Huh. So there's a mole. Oh well. It doesn't matter. You don't understand."

"Understand what?"

"Understand what it takes to protect the United States. You know that no other hurricanes have hit our shores since Hurricane Goliath made landfall, right? This country used to spend billions on disaster relief every year to clean up the multitude of messes made by hurricanes, but once we resettled everyone outside the perimeter of Hurricane Goliath, we haven't had to spend any money on that kind of disaster relief."

I set my jaw. "Who cares about that?"

"You should. You should also care about the fact that our country has made money on harvesting energy and water from the hurricane. Do you even know what your mom does? She heads up the energy farming operations."

My ears felt hot. No, I did not. I had never even asked what she did.

Chip sighed. "I have always loved your mom. Always. Since the first time I saw her in college. Doesn't that mean something?"

I shook my head. "So what? That gives you the right to swoop in now?"

He narrowed his eyes. "I'm running out of patience with you. If you loved your mom at all, you'd want her to be happy. That's all I want. She could have been happier if she had just married me instead of Jonah, but here we are. Finally making things right."

I couldn't believe he was saying this out loud. Or that there was no one else around to hear it. "Here's what I understand. I understand that you set my dad up to fail. And so will Mom, as soon as I tell her."

"She'll never believe you. Yes, my signature was on that document, but it proves nothing. Besides, you kids are all moving on, and I'm all she has left. Of course she'll turn to me."

I scoffed. "Think she'll still turn to you when we finally prove that the hurricane isn't natural? Because in a few weeks, we'll have proof of that too."

He froze. "What do you mean by that?"

The look on his face told me that the Storm Chasers were on the right track. Adrenaline surged through my veins. "I mean that after the Storm Chasers do what they have planned, we will show the world why the storm weakens every ten years. The truth will come out, and not even you can stop it. And I'll be able to hand my mom solid proof that you are directly responsible for ruining thousands of lives."

Chip crossed his arms and took one more step toward me, his voice even softer. "Are you sure you want to do that?"

"Why wouldn't I?"

"Because who do you think got Mason into the Air Force Academy? One word from me, and things might not go as well for him as he hopes."

I snorted. "I don't care. He told me he'd rather not have to think about me for the next few years, so he can deal with that on his own, just like he planned."

He narrowed his eyes. "Listen, girl. I'm on track to run for president in the next cycle. I need the funds from the energy harvest to support my campaign. Plus, a wife and family will make me much more relatable to the public."

I rolled my eyes. "That all sounds like a You Problem. I don't see how it is my job to give you a family so you can take over the United States."

Chip leaned in close enough that I almost gagged at the smell of his coffee breath. "I am the hurricane keeper, and I don't take threats against everything I've worked for lightly. If you blow this up, and your mom decides she doesn't want to be with me, then I see no reason why your mom needs to continue at USHA. I'm still in charge, and I can reorganize any department I want to. No one would bat an eye at me dismissing an older employee who is a drain on USHA's resources with her inflated salary and bloated family benefits. In fact, there's a hot young junior director who would be very grateful for a promotion right now."

I choked back a wave of nausea. "So much for your love."

He shrugged. "You'll learn someday that love is more than butterflies and stolen kisses. There are practical aspects to consider. I do love your mom, but I also have goals. And if those goals no longer include your family, well, then I'll have to tie up loose ends. I mean, how safe is Mella's new apartment complex, really? And I bet neither Penn nor Trig have even thought about home security."

I opened and closed my mouth, feeling like an idiot. I had no idea what to say. Of course, I had to tell my mom, but I didn't want her to lose her job. She loved her work. She mentioned more than once how connected to Dad she felt there.

Chip stepped back, a smile of satisfaction on his face. "Here's what we're going to do. I'm going to forget that your little storm friends have probably done something illegal to get the information you have, and you're going to forget this information altogether. You'll feel better once your mom and I are married, and you have full access to the White House. Trust me."

I just wanted him to go, so I pressed my lips together and nodded.

He reached out and squeezed my shoulder, and it took everything in me to not shrink away at his touch. Or to not punch him. "Good girl. Now, you really shouldn't be worrying about big things. Why don't you focus on your school? You're graduating soon, right?"

I stepped back and nodded, not trusting myself to say anything.

He smiled again. "Good. Okay, then. I'll see you later. I've invited your whole family over to my place for tacos and dominos. Sounds like fun, right?"

I forced a smile onto my face. "Oh yeah. Tons of fun. No cilantro for me, okay?"

Chip beamed. "You got it! See, we're going to make a great family."

I stepped onto the front porch and waved at him as he drove away. I kept myself in place, waving until he drove out of sight. Then I burst through the front door.

"Mom!"

CHAPTER 27

MOM POKED HER HEAD out of the kitchen. "Sheesh, Ashlyn. Why are you bellowing at six-thirty in the morning?"

"We've got to leave town."

She gave me a funny look. "What are you talking about? Come in. Chip just dropped off some donuts. He knew I was trying to cheer you up and brought these by as his contribution. Isn't that sweet? Oh, and he's invited us all over for tacos and games tonight. He knows the owner of that taco truck that was featured on the Food Channel App. What was the name of it?"

"Mom, you have to listen."

She chattered on as she headed back into the kitchen, pulling out plates and coffee mugs. "The Taco Trolley! That's it. Anyway, he reserved a food truck for us. Invite some of your friends. There will be way more tacos than our family can eat."

"Mom!"

She stopped and turned. Her hair was a disaster, she had no make-up on, and she wore her crusty, old, pink terrycloth bathrobe. The fact that Chip saw her in this just-from-bed state fanned the flames of my anger.

"What's wrong?"

"Listen to me. We have to leave town. Chip has threatened our whole family. He said that Mella's apartment isn't safe, and neither is Trig and Penn's."

She laughed a little. "Oh, honey. That makes no sense."

I took a deep breath and tried to start at the beginning. "The Storm Chasers found evidence that Chip set Dad's mission up to fail. I saw it. It was a list of supplies that Dad had requisitioned, and there were items crossed off. Things Dad needed. And Chip's signature was at the bottom."

Mom set down the coffee mugs she had pulled out. "Of course, his signature would be on it. You know he's been the director since before your dad's mission. He's always been great at administration. And changing a requisition before a mission isn't out of the ordinary."

I threw my hands up in the air. How could I make her see? "Well, I asked Chip about it. He didn't deny it! In fact, he said that you would have been happier if you had married him instead of Dad and that he's finally making things right."

She walked over and pulled me into a hug. "Sweetie, you must have misunderstood him. Chip was your dad's best friend. He didn't want Jonah going on the mission. He thought it was too dangerous. But he knew your dad wouldn't stop once he had an idea. He had to let him go, just like I did." Her voice had dropped to the soft tone she used to use when one of us kids was having a meltdown in a store.

She stroked my hair. "I promise you I will never put Chip above you, but I'm asking you to keep an open mind about us for a little while longer. This is my chance at an actual relationship, one with the potential to grow into something amazing based on our history and years of friendship." She twisted me around and looked into my face, her eyes full of compassion. "We understand it's going to take you some time to come to terms with this, and we're okay with that. Both Chip and I will take this as slow as you need. But please promise me you will give it a chance."

I tightened my grip on my com, ready to pull it out and show her the gross picture, when I stopped. Chip was right; Mom was going to choose him.

I let out a sigh. "Yeah, okay. I'll give it a chance, I promise."

She squeezed me and kissed the side of my head. "Thank you, Mini-Muffin."

I shrugged out of her grip. "I'm not saying that you get my stamp of approval, or that giving it a chance means I'll accept him tomorrow. It still might take me a long time."

She chuckled. "Noted. Now, do you want a donut?"

I shook my head. "No, I, I mean, Dasha and I didn't sleep much last night. I'm going to shower and take a nap."

"Did she make you feel better about Mason?"

This time, the sound of Mason's name made my stomach drop. When Chip brought him up, I was too mad to care. But the softness in Mom's voice pressed on the fresh bruise on my heart. The thing with Mason felt like it was a thousand years ago, yet just hearing her say his name brought back the pain in a rush. The raid on USHA and all the things I had learned had almost made me forget about him. For a brief second, I wondered what that meant. How real could our relationship have been if I had been able to put him out of my mind so quickly? But if that were true, why did hearing his name hurt so much?

My throat squeezed tight and tears pressed the back of my eyes. "That's going to take more time."

Mom nodded. "Yeah, it will. Listen, Ash. I know it never feels this way, but you have all the time in the world. Time to figure out your life, and time to imagine your life without Mason. You have plenty of time to adjust to all the changes around here, with your siblings and Chip. You really do. Take each day as it comes, alright?"

This time, I was the one to initiate the hug with my mom. I hugged her for a long moment. "Thanks, Mom."

She kissed my head once more, then gave me a pat on the backside. "Go shower, then sleep. We can go get lunch later."

I nodded and climbed the stairs to my room. I docked my com and sat on my bed, staring around my room. My eyes landed on the heart balloon, still dancing in the corner. I jumped up and squeezed it until it popped.

My brain was so jumbled. Nothing in my life was in my control anymore. I couldn't make my mom see the truth about Chip. Mason had shattered all the plans I had for the next year and beyond.

After my shower, I crawled into bed. I shut my eyes and tried to fall asleep, but I couldn't get the image of Chip leaning in close and threatening my family out of my head. I finally sat up, grabbed my com, and sent Luca a request for a video chat. Within seconds, his face filled the screen.

"What's up, Booker."

I rubbed my face, then flopped on my bed. "Everything is a mess."

"Spill."

"Don't be mad, but I confronted Chip."

"What? Are you kidding me?"

"I know! I'm sorry. But he was coming out of my house when I got home this morning, and I just got so mad that I blurted out that I had the proof."

He groaned. "What did he say?"

"Well, he didn't deny it."

"No, what did he say about the proof? Did he ask how you got it?"

"Yeah, but don't worry. I mean, I said the Storm Chasers, but I didn't name any names or say when or anything. I didn't tell him I was there." I swallowed hard. I had never seen Luca's face look so angry.

"Ashlyn, you could have ruined everything."

I shook my head. "No, don't worry. After literally threatening the safety of my family, Chip said that he would forget whatever illegal things the Storm Chasers did if I would drop the whole thing and never tell Mom."

"Then what did you do?"

"I told my mom."

"Ashlyn!"

A tear rolled down my face. "Don't worry, she didn't believe me. So nothing will come of it."

He sighed. "So, now what?"

"Now I want to go on the mission." The words popped out of my mouth almost on their own.

"Are you serious?"

I slowly nodded. Everything fell into place, and suddenly I knew what I wanted to do. "Yes, I'm serious. Finding my dad is the only way to fix any of this. I have to bring him back."

"How are you going to pull this off?"

I bit my lip. "The mission is the same week as my senior trip. I'll just go with the Storm Chasers instead of to Seattle. My family is expecting me to be gone, anyway."

He looked dubious. "Uh, the mission could take a lot longer than your senior trip. This is dangerous, Ash. It might even be a suicide mission."

I shrugged. "I have no other option. I can't live the life they're all planning me to live, with Chip in our family, and me going off to college by myself. And it doesn't matter if it takes longer. I'll already be gone; it's not like they'll be able to drag me back home."

He was quiet for a few minutes as he stared at me through the com screen. "Are you sure?"

Hope and excitement for the future washed over me for the first time since Mom had dropped the bombshell about Chip, and since Mason had made his declaration about going our separate ways. "I'm sure. I'm in."

"Okay. Pack your bags, Booker. We've got a train to catch."

Acknowledgements

I'm so thankful for all the people who gave me the encouragement and help needed to launch this story into the world:

My dad

The Scribes 209

My husband and girls

My Beta Readers: Jamie, Naomi, Kristen, Julane, Amanda, Megan

My Proofreaders: Mindy, Kara, Lori

The All Write Well Mentor team

You all make up the best tribe ever.

ABOUT THE AUTHOR

Victoria lives at the foot of the Rocky Mountains in Colorado with her husband, her three girls, and her unemployed housecat. She is a a full-fledged homebody, a so-so housekeeper, a mediocre musician, an amateur weather nerd, and has dreamed of writing her whole life.

Also by Victoria Kimble

Contemporary YA Fiction
The Main Dish

Faith- Based Middle Grade Contemporary Fiction
Soprano Trouble
Alto Secrets
Harmony Blues
Solo Disaster

Writing Prompts for Humans
Writing Prompts for the Hungry
Writing Prompts for the Animal Lover
Writing Prompts for the Nerds, Geeks, & Dorks
Writing Prompts for the Outdoorsy
Writing Prompts for the Suspicious